"So we agree to work as a team. For Tommy's sake."

"For Tommy's sake." Lucy took a step closer, and Niall inhaled the scents of baby powder and something slightly more exotic that didn't have anything to do with the infant she was pushing into his arms.

"Since I've convinced you that we're on the same side now, would you feel comfortable watching him for about ten minutes? That's all the time I'll need to freshen up and change so we're ready to go."

Her fingers caught for a moment between Tommy and the placket of Niall's shirt, and even through the pressed cotton, his stomach muscles clenched at the imprint of her knuckles brushing against his skin. But she pulled away to drape a burp rag over his shoulder, apparently unaware of his physiological reactions to her touch and scent.

APB: BABY

USA TODAY Bestselling Author

JULIE MILLER

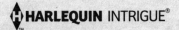

HARLEQUIN INTRIGUE®

For my husband, Scott E. Miller.

I'm so proud of you for writing your stories
and getting them published.

(Welcome to the joys and headaches of being an author.)

ISBN-13: 978-0-373-74963-8

APB: Baby

Copyright © 2016 by Julie Miller

Recycling programs
for this product may
not exist in your area.

Printed in U.S.A.

www.Harlequin.com

Julie Miller is an award-winning *USA TODAY* bestselling author of breathtaking romantic suspense—with a National Readers' Choice Award and a Daphne du Maurier Award, among other prizes. She has also earned an *RT Book Reviews* Career Achievement Award. For a complete list of her books, monthly newsletter and more, go to juliemiller.org.

Visit the Author Profile page at Harlequin.com for more titles.

CAST OF CHARACTERS

Dr. Niall Watson—A third generation cop, this medical examiner relies on his brain and his science to solve crimes, and understands dead bodies better than he does most people. But when he rescues an abandoned baby, his solitary, predictable life is turned upside down.

Lucy McKane—Her longtime crush on her sexy, reclusive neighbor erupts into something much deeper when Niall rescues the baby abandoned at her apartment.

Tommy—An innocent baby. Kidnapped and disposed of? Or given up as a last desperate measure to keep him out of harm's way?

Thomas Watson—Niall's father was forced to take early retirement because of an injury. But there's still KCPD blue running through his veins.

Thomas "Duff" Watson—Niall's older brother is short on patience. But he's the cop you want having your back in a fight.

Keir Watson—Niall's younger brother is the charmer of the family. But don't be fooled by the sweet talk. This detective is relentless when it comes to finding the truth.

Seamus Watson—The retired KCPD desk sergeant moved in when Niall's mother died. He's not about to let a crazed shooter force him to leave the family...permanently.

Millie Leighter—Cook, nanny, housekeeper. She raised the Watsons as if they were her own family.

Diana Kozlow—Is Lucy's former foster daughter repeating the mistakes Lucy once made?

Mikhail and Antony Staab—These brothers know something, but they aren't talking.

Roger Campbell—Lucy's ex-boyfriend just got out of prison. Is he still obsessed with ruining her life?

Alberta McKane—Lucy's mother. She and Lucy have never seen eye to eye.

Prologue

Dr. Niall Watson would rather be at the crime lab conducting an autopsy instead of standing at the altar, babysitting his brothers.

But saying no to his baby sister on the day of her wedding wasn't an option. Putting on the groomsman's suit and facing the crowd of smiles and tears that filled the church was as much a gift to Olivia and her fiancé as the sterling silver tableware he'd bought at the online department store where they'd registered. If Olivia, the youngest of the four Watson siblings, and the only sister, asked him to keep older brother Duff and younger brother Keir in line today, then Niall would do it. It was a brilliant strategy on her part, he silently admitted. Not only would their rowdier brothers be kept in check, but asking the favor of him was sure to keep Niall engaged in the ceremony. It was smart to give him a specific task to focus on so his mind didn't wander back to the dead body he'd analyzed yesterday morning at the lab in southeast Kansas City, and the follow-up notes he wanted to log in, or to the facts on a drowning victim he wanted to double-check before turning his findings over to the detectives supervising those particular cases.

As a third-generation cop in a close-knit family of law enforcement professionals, it was practically impossible not to be filled with investigative curiosity, or to have dedication and responsibility running through his veins. When it came to work and family, at any rate. And for Niall, there was nothing else. Work filled his life, and the Watson family filled his heart.

Except when they were screwing around— like Duff beside him, running his finger beneath the starched collar of his white shirt and grumbling something about Valentine's Day curses while he fiddled with the knot on his cherry-red tie. Or Keir, chattering up the aisle behind Niall, saying something outrageous enough to the bridesmaid he was escorting to make her giggle. Then Keir patted her hand on his arm and turned to wink at Millie, the family housekeeper-cook they'd all grown up with, as he passed the silver-haired woman in the second pew. The older woman blushed, and Keir blew her a kiss.

Niall adjusted the dark frames of his glasses and nailed Keir with a look warning him to let go of the bridesmaid, stop working the room and assume his place beside him as one of Gabe's groomsmen, already.

"Natalie is married to Liv's partner, you know." The tallest of the three brothers, Niall dropped his chin to whisper under his breath.

"Relax, charm-school dropout." Keir clapped Niall on the shoulder of the black tuxedo he wore, grinning as he stepped up beside him. "Young or old, married or not—it never hurts to be friendly."

Olivia might be the youngest of the four siblings, all third-generation law enforcement who served their city proudly. And she might be the only woman in the tight-knit Watson family since their mother's murder when Niall had barely been a teen. But there was no question that Liv ran the show. Despite Duff's tough-guy grousing or Keir's clever charm or Niall's own reserved, logical prowess, Olivia Mary Watson—soon to be Olivia Knight—had each of them, including their widowed father and grandfather, wrapped around her pretty little finger. If she asked Niall to keep their headstrong Irish family in line today, then he would do exactly that.

With Keir set for the moment, Niall angled his position toward the groom and best man Duff. He didn't need to adjust his glasses to see the bulge at the small of Duff's back beneath the tailored black jacket. Niall's nostrils flared with a patience-inducing breath before he whispered, "Seriously? Are you packing today?"

Duff's overbuilt shoulders shifted as he turned to whisper a response. "Hey. You wear your glasses every day, Poindexter. I wear my gun."

"I wasn't aware that you knew what the term *Poindexter* meant."

"I'm smarter than I look" was Duff's terse response.

Keir chuckled. "He'd have to be."

Duff's muscular shoulders shifted. "So help me, baby brother, if you give me any grief today, I will lay you out flat."

"Zip it. Both of you." Niall knew that he was quickly losing control of his two charges. He scowled at Keir. "You, mind your manners." When Duff went after the collar hugging his muscular neck again, Niall leaned in. "And you stop fidgeting like a little kid."

A curious look from the minister waiting behind them quieted all three brothers for the moment. With everything ready for their sister's walk down the aisle, the processional music started. Niall scanned the rest of the crowd as they rose to their feet. Their grandfather Seamus Watson hooked his cane over the railing as he stood in the front row. He winked one blue eye at Niall before pulling out his handkerchief and turning toward the aisle to dab at the tears he didn't want anybody to see.

And then Olivia and their father, Thomas Watson, appeared in the archway at the end of the aisle. A fist of rare sentimentality squeezed around Niall's heart.

His father was a relatively tall, stocky man. His black tuxedo and red vest and tie—an homage to the date, February 14—matched Niall's own attire. Niall knew a familiar moment of pride and respect as his father limped down the aisle, his shoulders erect despite the injury that had ended his career at KCPD at far too young an age. Other than the peppering of gray in Thomas's dark brown hair, Niall saw the same face when he looked into the mirror every morning.

But that wasn't what had him nodding his head in admiration.

His sister, that tough tomboy turned top-notch detective, the girl who'd never let three older brothers get the best of her, had grown up. Draped in ivory and sparkles, her face framed by the Irish lace veil handed down through their mother's side of the family, Olivia Watson was a beauty. Dark hair, blue eyes like his. But feminine, radiant. Her gaze locked on to Gabe at the altar, and she smiled. Niall hadn't seen a glimpse of his mother like that in twenty years.

"Dude," Duff muttered. He nudged the groom beside him. "Gabe, you are one lucky son of a—"

"Duff." Niall remembered his charge at the last moment and stopped his older brother from swearing in church.

Gabe sounded a bit awestruck himself as Olivia walked down the aisle. "I know."

"You'd better treat her right," Duff growled on a whisper.

Niall watched his brother's shoulders puff up. "We've already had this conversation, Duff. I'm convinced he loves her."

Gabe never took his eyes off Olivia as he inclined his head to whisper, "He does."

Keir, of course, wasn't about to be left out of the hushed conversation. "Anyway, Liv's made her choice. You think any one of us could change her mind? I'd be scared to try."

The minister hushed the lot of them as father and bride approached.

"Ah, hell," Duff muttered, looking up at the ceiling. He blinked rapidly, pinching his nose. The big guy was tearing up. "This is not happening to me."

"She looks the way I remember Mom," Keir said in a curiously soft voice.

Finally, the gravity of the day was sinking in and their focus was where it should be. Niall tapped Duff's elbow. "Do you have a handkerchief?"

"The rings are tied up in it."

"Here." Niall slipped his own white handkerchief to Duff, who quickly dabbed at his face. He nodded what passed for a thank-you and stuffed the cotton square into his pocket, steeling his jaw against the flare of emotion.

When Olivia arrived at the altar, she kissed their father, catching him in a tight hug before smiling at all three brothers. Duff sniffled again. Keir gave her a thumbs-up. Niall nodded approvingly. Olivia handed her bouquet off to her matron of honor, Ginny Rafferty-Taylor, and took Gabe's hand to face the minister.

The rest of the ceremony continued with everyone on their best behavior until the minister pronounced Gabe and Olivia husband and wife and announced, "You may now kiss the bride."

"Love you," Olivia whispered.

Gabe kissed her again. "Love you more."

"I now present Mr. and Mrs. Gabriel Knight."

Niall pondered the pomp and circumstance of this particular Valentine's Day as the guests applauded and the recessional music started. Logically, he knew the words Liv and Gabe had spoken and what they meant. But a part of him struggled to comprehend exactly how this sappy sort of pageantry equated to happiness and lifelong devotion. It was all a bit wearing, really. But if this was what Olivia wanted, he'd support her wholeheartedly and do whatever was necessary to make it happen.

Following Duff to the center of the aisle, Niall extended his arm to escort bridesmaid Katie Rinaldi down the marble steps. Despite his red-rimmed eyes, Thomas Watson smiled at each of his children. Niall smiled back.

Until he caught the glimpse of movement in the balcony at the back of the church. A figure in black emerged from the shadows beside a carved limestone buttress framing a row of organ pipes.

In a nanosecond frozen in time, a dozen observations blipped through Niall's mind. The organist played away upstairs, unaware of the intruder only a few yards from his position. The figure wore a ski mask and a long black coat. Clearly not a guest. Not church staff. The pews were filled with almost two hundred potential targets, many of them off-duty and retired police officers. His new brother-in-law had made more enemies than friends with his cutting-edge editorials. What did he want? Why was he here? Didn't have to be a cop hater with some kind of vendetta. Could be some crazy with nothing more in mind than making a deadly statement about a lost love or perceived injustice or mental illness.

The gleam of polished wood reflected the colored light streaming in through the balcony's stained-glass windows as the shooter pulled a rifle from his long cloak. Mauser hunting rifle. Five eight-millimeter rounds. He carried a second weapon, a semiautomatic pistol, strapped to his belt. That was enough firepower to do plenty of damage. Enough to kill far too many people.

Time righted itself as the analytical part of Niall's brain shut down and the years of training as a cop and medical officer kicked in. *Move!*

Niall shoved Katie to one side and reached for his father as the shooter took aim.

"Gun!" he shouted, pointing to the balcony as his fingers closed around the sleeve of Thomas Watson's jacket. "Get down!"

The *slap, slap, slap* of gunshots exploded through the church. The organ music clashed on a toxic chord and went silent. Wood splintered and flew like shrapnel. A vase at the altar shattered. Flower petals and explosions of marble dust rained in the air.

"Everybody down!" Duff ordered, drawing the pistol from the small of his back. He dropped to one knee on the opposite side of the aisle and raised his weapon. "Drop it!"

"I'm calling SWAT." Keir ducked between two pews, pulling his phone from his jacket as he hugged his arms around Natalie Fensom and Millie Leighter.

Niall saw Gabe Knight slam his arms around Liv and pull her to the marble floor beneath his body. Guests shouted names of loved ones. A child cried out in fear, and a mother hastened to comfort him. Warnings not to panic, not to run, blended together with the screams and tromping footfalls of people doing just that.

"I've got no shot," Duff yelled, pushing to a

crouching position as the shooter dropped his spent rifle and pulled his pistol. Niall heard Keir's succinct voice reporting to dispatch. With a nod from Katie that she was all right and assurance that her husband was circling around the outside aisle to get to her, Niall climbed to his knees to assess the casualties. He caught a glimpse of Duff and a couple of other officers zigzagging down the aisle through the next hail of bullets and charging out the back of the sanctuary. "Get down and stay put!"

Niall squeezed his father's arm. He was okay. He glanced back at the minister crouched behind the pulpit. He hadn't been hit, either. The man in the balcony shouted no manifesto, made no threat. He emptied his gun into the sanctuary, grabbed his rifle and scrambled up the stairs toward the balcony exit. He was making a lot of noise and doing a lot of damage and generating a lot of terror. But despite the chaos, he wasn't hitting anyone. What kind of maniac set off this degree of panic without having a specific—

"Niall!" His grandfather's cane clattered against the marble tiles. Niall was already peeling off his jacket and wadding it up to use as a compress as Thomas Watson cradled the eighty-year-old man in his arms and gently low-ered him to the floor. "Help me, son. Dad's been shot."

Chapter One

Niall stepped off the elevator in his condominium building to the sound of a baby crying.

His dragging feet halted as the doors closed behind him, his nostrils flaring as he inhaled a deep, weary breath, pulled the phone from his ear and checked his watch. Two in the morning.

Great. Just great. He had nothing against babies—he knew many of them grew into very fine adults. But he'd been awake going on twenty hours now, had been debriefed six ways to Sunday by cops and family and medical staff alike, hadn't even had a chance to change his ruined fancy clothes, and was already feeling sleep deprived by switching off his typical nocturnal work schedule to be there for Liv's wedding. No way was he going to catch a couple hours of much-needed shut-eye before he headed back to the hospital later this morning.

He put the phone back to his ear and finished the conversation with Duff. "You know we can't investigate this shooting personally. There's a huge conflict of interest since the victim is family."

"Then I'm going to find out which detectives caught the case and make sure they keep us in the loop."

"You do that. And I'll keep track of any evidence that comes through the lab."

"We'll find this guy." Duff's pronouncement was certain. "Get some sleep, Niall."

"You, too." Niall disconnected the call, knowing he couldn't comply with his older brother's directive.

But it wasn't the pitiful noise of the infant's wails, nor the decibel level of distress that solid walls could only mute, that would keep him awake.

His brain's refusal to let a question go unanswered was going to prevent his thoughts from quieting until he could solve the mystery of where that crying baby had come from and to whom the child belonged. As if the events of the day—with his grandfather lying in intensive care and an unidentified shooter on the loose in Kansas City—weren't enough to keep him from sleeping, now a desperately unhappy infant and Niall's own curiosity over the un-expected sound were probably going to eat up whatever downtime he had left tonight. Curs-ing that intellectual compulsion, Niall rolled his kinked-up neck muscles and started down the hallway.

Considering three of the six condos on this floor were empty, a retired couple in their sev-enties lived in one at the far end of the hall and Lucy McKane, who lived across the hall from his place, was a single like himself, the crying baby posed a definite mystery. Perhaps the Lo-gans were babysitting one of the many grand-children they liked to talk about. Either that or Lucy McKane had company tonight. Could she be watching a friend's child? Dating a single dad who'd brought along a young chaperone? Letting a well-kept secret finally reveal itself?

Although they'd shared several early-morn-ing and late-night chats, he and Lucy had never gotten much beyond introductions and polite conversations about the weather and brands of detergent. Just because he hadn't seen a ring on her finger didn't mean she wasn't attached to someone. And even though he struggled with interpersonal relationships, he wasn't so clue-less as to think she had to be married or seeing someone in order to get pregnant.

So the crying baby was most likely hers.

Good. Mystery solved. Niall pulled his keys from his pocket as he approached his door. Sleep might just happen.

Or not.

The flash of something red and shiny in the carpet stopped Niall in the hallway between their two doors. He stooped down to retrieve a minuscule shard of what looked like red glass. Another mystery? Didn't building maintenance vacuum out here five days a week? This was a recent deposit and too small to identify the source. A broken bottle? Stained glass? The baby wailed through the door off to his right, and Niall turned his head. He hadn't solved anything at all.

Forget the broken glass. Where and when did Lucy McKane get a baby?

He'd never seen her coming home from a date before, much less in the company of a man with a child. And he was certain he hadn't noticed a baby bump on her. Although she could have been hiding a pregnancy, either intentionally or not. He generally ran into her in the elevator when she was wearing bulky hand-knit sweaters or her winter coat, or in the gym downstairs, where she sported oversize T-shirts with one silly or motivational message or another. And then there were those late-night visits in the basement laundry room, where there'd been clothes baskets and tables between them to mask her belly. Now that he thought about it, Lucy McKane wore a lot of loose-fitting clothes. Her fashion choices tended to emphasize her generous breasts and camouflage the rest of her figure. He supposed she could have been carrying a baby one of those late nights when they'd discussed fabric softener versus dryer sheets, and he simply hadn't realized it.

If that was the case, though, why hadn't he seen the child or heard it crying before tonight? The woman liked to talk. Wouldn't she have announced the arrival of her child?

Maybe he'd rethink other options. It was the wee hours after Valentine's Day. She could be watching the child for a friend out on an overnight date. But why hadn't Lucy gone out for Valentine's Day? The woman was pretty in an unconventional kind of way, if one liked a cascade of dark curls that were rarely tamed, green eyes that were slightly almond shaped and the apple cheeks and a pert little nose that would make her look eternally young. She made friends easily enough, judging by her ability to draw even someone like him into random conversations. And she was certainly well-spoken—at least when it came to washing clothes and inclement weather, gossip about the building's residents and the news of the day. So why wasn't a woman like that taken? Where was *her* date?

And why was he kneeling here in a stained, wrinkled tuxedo and eyes that burned with fatigue, analyzing the situation at all? He needed sleep, desperately. Otherwise, his mind wouldn't be wandering like this.

"Let it go, Watson," he chided himself, pushing to his feet.

Niall turned to the door marked 8C and inserted his key into the lock. At least he could clearly pinpoint the source of the sound now. The noise of the unhappy baby from behind Lucy McKane's door was jarring to his weary senses. He was used to coming home in shrouded silence when his swing shift at the medical examiner's office ended. Most of the residents in the building were asleep by then. He respected their need for quiet as much as he craved it himself. He never even turned on the radio or TV. He'd brew a pot of decaf and sit down with a book or his reading device until he could shut down his thoughts from the evening and turn in for a few hours of sleep. Sending a telepathic brain wave to the woman across the hall to calm her child and allow them all some peace, he went inside and closed the door behind him.

After hanging up his coat in the front closet, Niall switched on lamps and headed straight to the wet bar, where he tossed the sliver of glass onto the counter, unhooked the top button of his shirt and poured himself a shot of whiskey. Sparing a glance for the crimson smears that stained his jacket sleeve and shirt cuffs, he raised his glass to the man he'd left sleeping in the ICU at Saint Luke's Hospital. Only when his younger brother had come in to spell him for a few hours after Keir and Duff had hauled Liv and her new husband, Gabe, off to a fancy hotel where they could spend their wedding night—in lieu of the honeymoon they'd postponed—had Niall left Seamus Watson's side. "This one's for you, Grandpa."

Niall swallowed the pungent liquor in one gulp, savoring the fire burning down his gullet and chasing away the chill of a wintry night and air-conditioned hospital rooms that clung to every cell of his body. It had been beyond a rough day. His grandfather was a tough old bird, and Niall had been able to stanch the bleeding and stabilize him at the church well enough to keep shock from setting in. He'd ridden with the paramedics to the hospital, and they had done their job well, as had the ER staff. But the eighty-year-old man had needed surgery to repair the bleeders from the bullet that had fractured his skull and remove the tiny bone fragments that had come dangerously close to entering his brainpan and killing him.

Although the attending surgeon and neurologist insisted Seamus was now guardedly stable and needed to sleep, the traumatic brain injury had done significant damage. Either due to the wound itself, or a resulting stroke, he'd lost the use of his left arm and leg, had difficulty speaking and limited vision in his left eye. Seamus was comfortable for now, but age and trauma had taken a toll on his body and he had a long road to recovery ahead of him. And as Niall had asked questions of the doctors and hovered around the nurses and orderlies while they worked, he couldn't help but replay those minutes at the end of the wedding over and over in his head.

Had Seamus Watson been the shooter's intended target? And since the old man seemed determined to live, would the shooter be coming back to finish the job? Was Grandpa safe? Or was his dear, funny, smarter-than-the-rest-of-them-put-together grandfather a tragic victim of collateral damage?

If so, who had the man with all those bullets really been after? Why plan the attack at the church? Was the Valentine's Day date significant? Was his goal to disrupt the wedding, make a statement against KCPD, or simply to create chaos and validate his own sense of power? Even though others had been hurt by minor shrapnel wounds, and one man had suffered a mild heart attack triggered by the stress of the situation, the number of professionally trained guests had kept the panic to a minimum. So who was the shooter? Duff said he'd chased the perp up onto the roof, but then the man had disappeared before Duff or any of the other officers in pursuit could reach him. What kind of man planned his escape so thoroughly, yet failed to hit anyone besides the Watson patriarch? And if Seamus was the intended target, what was the point of all the extra damage and drama?

And could Niall have stopped the tragedy completely if he'd spotted the man in the shadows a few seconds sooner? He scratched his fingers through the short hair that already stood up in spikes atop his head after a day of repeating the same unconscious habit. Niall prided himself on noting details. But today he'd missed the most important clue of his life until it was too late.

His brothers would be looking into Seamus's old case files and tracking down any enemies that their grandfather might have made in his career on the force, despite his retirement fifteen years earlier. Duff and Keir would be following up any clues found by the officers investigating the case that could lead to the shooter's identity and capture. Frustratingly, Niall's involvement with finding answers was done—unless one of his brothers came up with some forensic evidence he could process at the lab. And even then, Niall's expertise was autopsy work. He'd be doing little more than calling in favors to speed the process and following up with his coworkers at the crime lab. Although it galled him to take a backseat in the investigation, logic indicated he'd better serve the family by taking point on his grandfather's care and recovery so his brothers could focus on tracking down the would-be assassin.

Niall picked up the Bushmills to pour himself a second glass, but the muted cries of the baby across the hall reminded him that he wasn't the only one dealing with hardship tonight, and he returned the bottle to the cabinet.

He wanted to have a clear head in the morning when he returned to the hospital for a follow-up report on his grandfather. He could already feel his body surrendering to the tide of fatigue, and despite his unsettling thoughts, he loathed the idea of dulling his intellect before he found the answers he needed. So he set the glass in the sink and moved into the kitchen to start a small pot of decaf.

While the machine hissed and bubbled, he shrugged out of the soiled black tuxedo jacket and draped it over the back of a chair. After pulling out the rented tie he'd folded up into a pocket and laying it over the coat, he went to work unbuttoning the cherry-red vest he wore. Typically, he didn't wear his gun unless he was out in the field at a crime scene. But with his family threatened and too many questions left unanswered, he'd had Duff unlock it from the glove compartment of Niall's SUV and bring it to the hospital, where he'd strapped it on. Niall halted in the middle of unhooking his belt to remove it, opting instead to roll up his sleeves and leave himself armed. Until he understood exactly what was going on, it would be smart to keep that protection close at hand.

Whether it was the gun's protection, the re-sumption of his nightly routine or the discordant noise from across the hall receding, Niall braced his hands against the edge of the sink to stretch his back and drop his chin, letting his eyes close as the tension in him gave way to weariness.

The distant baby's cries shortened like staccato notes, as if the child was running out of the breath or energy to maintain the loud wails. Maybe Miss McKane was finally having some success in quieting the infant. Despite how much she liked to talk, she seemed like a capable sort of woman. Sensible, too. She carried her keys on a ring with a small pepper spray canister in her hand each time he saw her walking to or from her car in the parking lot. She wore a red stocking hat on her dark curly hair when the weather was cold and wet to conserve body heat. She sorted her jeans and towels from her whites and colors. Okay, so maybe she wasn't completely practical. Why did a woman need so many different types of underwear, anyway? Cotton briefs, silky long johns, lacy bras in white and tan and assorted pastels, animal prints...

Niall's eyes popped open when he realized he was thinking about Lucy McKane's underwear. And not folded up in her laundry basket or tucked away in a dresser drawer, either.

Good grief. Imagining his neighbor's pale skin outlined in that tan-and-black leopard-print duo he'd found so curiously distracting tossed on top of her folding pile was hardly appropriate. Exhaustion must be playing tricks on him. Pushing away from the sink, Niall clasped his glasses at either temple and adjusted the frames on his face, as if the action could refocus the wayward detour of his thoughts. It was irritating that he could be so easily distracted by curves and cotton or shards of glass or mystery babies who were none of his business when he wanted to concentrate on studying the events before, during and after the shooting at the wedding. Perhaps he should have skipped the shot of whiskey and gone straight for the steaming decaf he poured into a mug.

He added a glug of half-and-half from the fridge and carried the fragrant brew to the bookshelf in the living room, where he pulled out a medical volume to look up some of the details relating to his grandfather's condition. He savored the reviving smell of the coffee before taking a drink and settling into the recliner beside the floor lamp.

Niall had barely turned the first page when the infant across the hall found his second wind and bellowed with a high-pitched shriek that nearly startled him into spilling his drink.

Enough. Was the child sick? Had he completely misjudged Lucy McKane's competence? Niall set his book and mug on the table beside him and pushed to his feet. Maybe the muted noise of a baby crying didn't bother anybody else. Maybe no one else could hear the child's distress. He was so used to the building being quiet at this hour that maybe he was particularly sensitive to the muffled sounds. And maybe he'd come so close to losing someone he loved today that he just didn't have the patience to deal with a neighbor who couldn't respect his need for a little peace and quiet and time to regroup.

In just a few strides he was out the door and across the hall, knocking on Lucy McKane's front door. When there was no immediate response, he knocked harder. "Miss McKane? Do you know how late it is? Some of us are trying to sleep." Well, he hadn't been. But it wasn't as though he could if he even wanted to with that plaintive racket filtering through the walls. "Miss McKane?"

Niall propped his hands at his waist, waiting several seconds before knocking again. "Miss McKane?" Why didn't the woman answer her door? She couldn't be asleep with the baby crying like that, could she? In a heartbeat, Niall's irritation morphed into concern at the lack of any response. That could explain the infant's distress. Maybe Lucy McKane *couldn't* help the child. He flattened his palm against the painted steel and pounded again. "Miss McKane? It's Niall Watson from across the hall. Are you in there? Is everything all right?"

He reached down to jiggle the knob, but the cold metal twisted easily in his hand and the door creaked open a couple of inches.

Niall's suspicion radar went on instant alert. What woman who lived alone in the city didn't keep her door locked?

"Miss McKane?" he called out. But his only response was the even louder decibel level of the crying baby. He squinted the scratches on the knob into focus and quickly pulled his phone from his pocket to snap a picture. A familiar glint of red glass wedged between the frame and catch for the dead bolt higher up caught his eye. The tiny shattered orb looked like the source of the shard he'd found in the carpet.

Finally. Answers. But he didn't like them.

There were deeper gouges in the wood trim around it, indicating that both locks had been forced. His brain must have been half-asleep not to have suspected earlier that something was seriously wrong. Niall snapped a second picture. "Miss McKane? Are you all right?"

For a few seconds, the concerns of his Hippocratic oath warred with the procedure drilled into him by his police training. His brother Duff would muscle his way in without hesitation, while Keir would have a judge on speed dial, arranging an entry warrant. Niall weighed his options. The baby was crying and Lucy wasn't answering. His concern for the occupants' safety was reason enough to enter a potentially dangerous situation despite risking any kind of legalities. Tonight he'd forgo caution and follow his older brother's example.

"Hold tight, little one," he whispered, unstrapping his holster and pulling the service weapon from his belt. Although he was more used to handling a scalpel than a Glock, as a member of the KCPD crime lab, he'd been trained and certified to use the gun.

He held it surely as he nudged open the broken door. "Miss McKane? It's Niall Watson with the KCPD crime lab. I'm concerned for your safety. I'm coming in."

The mournful wails of a baby crying itself into exhaustion instantly grew louder on this side of the walls separating their living spaces. He backed against the door, closing it behind him as he cradled the gun between both hands. A dim light in the kitchen provided the only illumination in the condo that mirrored the layout of his own place. Allowing his vision to adjust to the dim outlines of furniture and doorways, Niall waited before advancing into the main room. He checked the closet and powder room near the entryway before moving through the living and dining rooms. Empty. No sign of Lucy McKane anywhere. No blood or signs of an accident or struggle of any sort, either. In fact, the only things that seemed out of place were the bundles of yarn, patterns and knitting needles that had been dumped out of their basket onto the coffee table and strewn across the sofa cushions and area rug.

He found the baby in the kitchen, fastened into a carrier that sat on the peninsula countertop, with nothing more than the glow of an automatic night-light beside the stove to keep him company. A half-formed panel of gray knitted wool hung from the baby's toes, as if he'd once been covered with it but had thrashed it aside.

Niall flipped on the light switch and circled around the peninsula, plucking the makeshift blanket off and laying it on the counter. "You're a tiny thing to be making all that noise. You all alone in here? Do you know where your mama is?"

The kid's red face lolled toward Niall's hushed voice. It shook and batted its little fists before cranking up to wail again. Niall didn't need to take a second whiff to ascertain at least one reason why the baby was so unhappy. But a quick visual sweep didn't reveal any sign of a diaper bag or anything to change it into besides the yellow outfit it wore. Had Lucy McKane left the child alone to go make a supply run?

Niall moved the gun down to his side and touched the baby's face. Feverish. Was the kid sick? Or was that what this ceaseless crying did to someone who was maybe only a week or so old?

The infant's cries sputtered into silent gasps as Niall splayed his fingers over its heaving chest. Not unlike his grandfather's earlier that day, the baby's heart was racing. A quick check farther down answered another question for him. "You okay, little man?"

How long had he been left unattended like this?

And where was Lucy? There was no sign of her in the kitchen, either, despite the dirty dishes in the sink and what looked like a congealed glob of cookie dough in the stand mixer beside it. It seemed as though she'd left in the middle of baking a dessert. Why hadn't she completed the task? Where had she gone? What had called her away? And, he thought, with a distinct note of irritation filtering into his thought process, why hadn't she taken the baby with her?

"Hold on." Niall's gaze was drawn to a screwdriver on the counter that didn't look like any piece of cooking equipment he'd ever seen his late mother or Millie Leighter use.

After a couple of silent sobs vibrated through the infant's delicate chest, Niall pulled his hand away. Tuning out the recommencing wail, he opened two drawers before he found a plastic bag and used it to pick up the tool. The handle was an absurd shade of pink with shiny baubles glued around each end of the grip. He rolled it in his hand until he found what he suspected he might—an empty space in the circle of fake stones. Niall glanced back through the darkened apartment. The bead stuck in the frame of her door suddenly made sense. But even if his neighbor had lost her key and had to break into her own place, she'd turn on the lights once she got in. There'd be signs of her being here. And she'd damn well take care of the baby.

Unless she wasn't the one who'd broken in.

"Don't go anywhere," he ordered needlessly. Wrapping the screwdriver securely in the bag, Niall slipped it into his pocket and clasped the gun between his hands again. "I'll be right back."

A quick inspection through the bedroom and en suite showed no sign of Lucy McKane there, either. He didn't see her purse anywhere, and her winter coat and accoutrements were missing from the front closet. There was no baby paraphernalia in any of the rooms.

Had she been kidnapped? What kind of kidnapper would leave evidence like the screwdriver behind? Had she been robbed? Nothing here seemed disturbed beyond the topsy-turvy knitting basket, and anything of typical value to a thief—her flat-screen TV, a laptop computer—was still here.

More unanswered questions. Niall's concern reverted to irritation.

This child had been abandoned. Lucy McKane was gone, and the woman had a lot of explaining to do.

Niall was surprisingly disappointed to learn that she was the type of woman to leave an infant alone to run errands or enjoy a date. She was a free spirit, certainly, with her friendly smile and ease at striking up conversations with neighbors she barely knew and ownership of far too many pairs of panties. But she'd told him she was a social worker, for pity's sake. He wouldn't have pegged her to be so self-absorbed and reckless as to leave a child in an unlocked apartment—to leave the child, period. *If* she'd left by choice.

With the mandate of both his badge and his medical degree, and three generations of protecting those who couldn't protect themselves bred into him, Niall could not walk out that door and abandon this baby himself. So, understanding as much about children as his medical books could teach, he tucked his gun into its holster, pulled his phone from his pocket and picked up the baby in its carrier. He spared a glance at the soft wood around the deadbolt catch, debating whether or not he should retrieve the decorative bead jammed there or report Lucy as a missing person. Making the crying infant his first priority, Niall closed the door behind him and carried the baby into his apartment before dialing the most knowledgeable parent he knew.

The phone picked up on the third ring. "Niall?"

"Dad." He set the carrier on the island in his

own kitchen and opened a drawer to pull out two clean dish towels. A quick glance at his watch indicated that perhaps he should have thought this through better. "Did I wake you?"

"It's three in the morning, son. Of course you did." Thomas Watson pushed the grogginess from his voice. "Are you still at the hospital? Has there been a change in Dad's condition?"

"No. The doctors are keeping Grandpa lightly sedated. Keir will stay with him until one of us relieves him in the morning."

"Thank God one of my boys is a doctor and that you were there to give him the treatment he needed immediately. We should be giving thanks that he survived and no one else was seriously injured. But knowing that the bastard who shot him is still…" Thomas Watson's tone changed from dark frustration to curious surprise. "Do I hear a baby crying?"

Niall strode through his apartment, retrieving a towel and washcloth along with the first-aid kit and a clean white T-shirt from his dresser. "Yes. Keir will contact me if there is any change in Grandpa's condition. I told Grandpa one or all of us would be by to see him in the morning, that the family would be there for him 24/7. I'm not sure he heard me, though."

"Dad heard you, I'm sure." Niall could hear

his father moving now, a sure sign that the former cop turned investigative consultant was on his feet and ready for Niall to continue. "Now go back to the other thing. Why do you have a baby?"

Niall had returned to the kitchen to run warm water in the sink. "Can I ask you a favor?"

"Of course, son."

"Dad, I need newborn diapers, bottles and formula. A clean set of clothes and some kind of coat or blanket or whatever babies need when it's cold. A car seat, too, if you can get your hands on one at this time of night. I'll reimburse you for everything, of course." Niall put the phone on speaker and spread a thick towel out on the counter, pausing for a moment to assess the locking mechanism before unhooking the baby and lifting him from the carrier. "Good Lord, you don't weigh a thing."

"The baby, Niall." That tone in his father's voice had always commanded an answer. "Is there something you need to tell me?"

"It's the neighbor's kid," Niall explained. "I'd get the items myself, but I don't have a car seat and can't leave him alone. Oh, get something for diaper rash, too. He needs a bath. I can use a clean dish towel to cover him up until you get here, although I don't have any safety pins.

Do you think medical tape would work to hold a makeshift diaper on him until you arrive?"

"You're babysitting? I never thought I'd see the day—"

"Just bring me the stuff, Dad."

Another hour passed before Thomas Watson arrived with several bags of supplies. His father groused about bottles looking different from the time Olivia had been the last infant in the house and how there were far too many choices for a feeding regimen. But between the two of them, they got the baby diapered, fed and dressed in a footed sleeper that fit him much better than Niall's long T-shirt. At first, Niall was concerned about the infant falling asleep before finishing his first bottle. But he roused enough for Thomas to coax a healthy burp out of him before drinking a little more and crashing again. Niall was relieved to feel the baby's temperature return to normal and suspected the feverish state had been pure stress manifesting itself.

The infant boy was sleeping in Thomas Watson's lap as the older man dozed in the recliner, and Niall was reviewing a chapter on pediatric medicine when he heard the ding of the elevator at the end of the hallway. He closed the book and set it on the coffee table, urging his waking father to stay put while he went to the door.

He heard Lucy McKane's hushed voice mumbling something as she approached and then a much louder, "Oh, my God. I've had a break-in."

Niall swung open his door and approached the back of the dark-haired woman standing motionless before her apartment door. She had turned silent, but he knew exactly what to say. "Miss McKane? You and I need to talk."

Chapter Two

"The man wasn't following me," Lucy chanted under her breath for the umpteenth time since parking her car downstairs. She stepped off the elevator into the shadowed hallway, trying to convince herself that the drunken ape who'd offered to rock her world down on Carmody Street wasn't the driver of the silver sports car she'd spotted in her rearview mirror less than a block from her condominium building a few minutes earlier. "He wasn't following me."

Maybe if she hadn't spotted a similar car veering in and out of the lane behind her on Highway 71, she wouldn't be so paranoid. Maybe if her voice mail at work didn't have a message from her ex-boyfriend Roger that was equal parts slime and threat and booze.

"Guess what, sweet thing. I'm out. And I'm coming to see you."

Maybe if it wasn't so late, maybe if she'd felt safe in that run-down part of Kansas City, maybe if she wasn't so certain that something terrible had happened to Diana Kozlow, her former foster daughter, who'd called her out of the blue yesterday after more than a year of no contact—maybe if the twenty-year-old would answer her stupid phone any one of the dozen times Lucy had tried to call her back— she wouldn't feel so helpless or alone or afraid.

Fortunately, the silver car had driven past when she'd turned in to the gated parking garage. But the paranoia and a serious need to wash the man's grimy hands off her clothes and skin remained. "He was *not* following me."

She glanced down at the blurred picture she'd snapped through her rear window the second time the silver roadster had passed a car and slipped into the lane behind her on 71. Her pulse pounded furiously in her ears as she slipped the finger of her glove between her teeth and pulled it off her right hand to try and enlarge the picture and get a better look at the driver or read a possible license plate. Useless. No way could she prove the Neanderthal or Roger or anyone else had followed her after leaving the rattrap apartment building on Carmody, which was the last address she had for Diana. Not that it had been a productive visit. The super had refused to speak to her, and the only resident who would answer her questions about Diana was an elderly woman who couldn't remember a young brunette woman living in the building, and didn't recognize her from the old high school photo Lucy had shown her. Ape man had been willing to tell her anything—in exchange for stepping into the alley with him for a free grope.

None of which boded well for the life Diana had forged for herself after aging out of the foster system and leaving Lucy's home. Lucy swiped her finger across the cell screen to pull up the high school photo of the dark-haired beauty she'd thought would be family—or at least a close friend—forever. "Oh, sweetie, what have you gotten yourself into?" she muttered around the red wool clasped between her teeth.

She glanced back at the elevator door, remembered the key card required to get into the building lobby.

"Okay. The creeper didn't follow me," she stated with as much conviction as she could muster. "And I will find you, Diana."

She was simply going to have to get a few

hours' sleep and think this through and start her search again tomorrow. Except...

Lucy pulled up short when she reached the door to 8D. The late-night chill that had iced her skin seeped quickly through the layers of clothing she wore.

"Oh, my God. I've had a break-in."

So much for feeling secure.

The wood around the locks on her apartment door was scratched and broken. The steel door itself drifted open with barely a touch of her hand. Lucy retreated half a step and pulled up the keypad on her phone to call the police. After two previous calls about Diana's failure to show up for lunch or return her calls, they were probably going to think she was a nutcase to call a third time in fewer than twenty-four hours.

"Miss McKane? You and I need to talk."

Lucy's fear erupted in a startled yelp at the succinct announcement. She swung around with her elbow at the man's deep voice behind her, instinctively protecting herself.

Instead of her elbow connecting with the man's solar plexus, five long fingers clamped like a vise around her wrist and she was pushed up against the wall by a tall, lanky body. Her phone popped loose from her slippery grip and bounced across the carpet at her feet. Her heart thumped in her chest at the wall of heat trapping her there, and the loose glove she'd held between her teeth was caught between her heaving breasts and the broad expanse of a white tuxedo shirt. What the devil? Diana was missing, and she had no idea why her tall, lanky neighbor was glowering down at her through those Clark Kent glasses he wore.

"Wow," she gasped, as the frissons of fear evaporated once she recognized him. No one else roamed the hallways this time of night except for him. She should have known better. "Sorry I took a swing at you, Dr. Watson." She couldn't even summon the giggly response she usually had when she said his name and conjured up thoughts of medical sidekicks and brainy British detectives. Not when she was embarrassingly aware of his hard runner's body pressed against hers. Nothing to giggle about there. The full-body contact lasted another awkward moment. "I didn't hurt you, did I?"

"Of course not." Once he seemed certain she recognized him as a friend and didn't have to defend himself, Niall Watson released his grip on her arm and stepped away, leaving a distinct chill in place of that surprising male heat that had pinned her to the wall. "I shouldn't have startled you."

"I thought you…were someone else."

"Who? Were you expecting someone?"

"I, um…" She wasn't about to explain her paranoid suspicions about ape man or Roger and the silver car, so she covered her rattled state by stooping down to retrieve her glove and phone. "Sorry if I woke you. I've had a break-in. I thought this was supposed to be a secure building in a safe neighborhood, but I guess there's no place that's truly safe if someone is determined to get to you. That's probably why I swung first. A girl has to take care of herself, you know. I'd better call the police."

Niall Watson's long fingers reached her phone first. He scooped it up and tapped the screen clear. "A 911 call won't be necessary."

Frowning at his high-handedness, Lucy tilted her face up. "Why not?" She was halfway to making eye contact when she saw the crimson spots staining his rolled-up sleeve. She stuffed her loose glove into her pocket, along with her phone, and touched her fingertip to the red stains on the wrinkled white cotton clinging to his long, muscular forearm. There were more droplets of blood on the other sleeve, too. Irritation vanished, and she piled concern for him onto the fears that had already worn her ragged today.

"Are you hurt? Did you stop the intruder?" She grasped his wrist in her hand, much the same way he'd manhandled her, and twisted it to find the wound. Despite the tempting awareness at his toasty-warm skin beneath her chilled fingers, she was more interested in learning what had happened. She knew he was affiliated with the police. Had he stepped in to prevent a burglar from ransacking her place? Had Roger followed his release from prison with a road trip to Kansas City? Had Diana shown up while she was searching the city for her? Now she looked up and met those narrowed cobalt eyes. "Have you already called for help? Do I need to take you to the hospital?"

A dark eyebrow arched above the rim of his glasses before he glanced down to see the source of her concern. Blinking away his apparent confusion, he pulled out of her grip to splay his fingers at his waist. "This isn't my blood."

"Then whose…?" His stance drew her attention to the holster strapped to his belt. Had she ever seen Niall Watson wearing a gun before? His badge, yes. But she'd never seen the erudite professional looking armed and dangerous the way he did tonight. Had he just come from a crime scene? "You wore a tuxedo to work?" Wait. Not his blood. That meant… A stone of dread plummeted into Lucy's stomach. Was that Diana's blood? "Oh, God." Before he could say anything, she spun around and shoved open the door to her apartment. "Diana?" Niall Watson was a doctor. But he wasn't hurt. That meant someone else was. "Diana? Are you here?"

She called out again for some sign that the young woman she'd been searching the city for all day and night had somehow shown up here.

The vise clamped over her wrist again and pulled her back to the door. "Miss McKane."

"Let go of me." She yanked her arm free and charged toward the mess on the couch. "Diana?" She paused a moment to sift through the pile of unraveling yarn and interrupted projects before snatching up the overturned basket and inspecting the insides. Lucy always kept a twenty or two hidden beneath her work. The only other person who knew where she stockpiled for a rainy day was Diana. "She was here. She took the cash," she whispered, her sense of dread growing exponentially.

"So it *was* a robbery?"

She startled at the deep voice beside her. "What? No. I would gladly give her the money."

"Give who the money?"

"Diana?" Lucy tossed the basket onto the couch and took off for the light in the kitchen.

But she hadn't taken two steps before Niall Watson's arm cinched around her waist and pulled her back against his chest. "Miss McKane. There's nothing for you to see here. I need you to come with me."

She gasped at the unexpected contact with a muscled torso and the surprising warmth that seemed to surround her instantly and seep through the layers of coat and clothing she wore. "Nothing? I have to…" For a split second, her fingers tightened their grip around the arm at her waist, needing his strength. She'd had a bad feeling all day. Diana Kozlow hadn't shown up for a long-overdue lunch and gab session. And then that phone call…

If the answer was here—even one she didn't want to be true—Lucy had to see for herself. With a renewed sense of urgency, she pushed the doctor's arm and body heat away and turned. "You need to stop grabbing me, Doctor. I appreciate your concern, but I have to—"

She shoved at his chest, but he released her waist only to seize her by the shoulders. He squeezed enough to give her a little shake and hunched his face down to hers. "Lucy. If you would please listen."

Lucy? Her struggles stilled as she assessed the stern expression stamped on his chiseled features. When had her taciturn neighbor ever addressed her as anything but a polite *Miss McKane*? That couldn't be good. The tight grip on her upper arms and the piercing intensity of those blue eyes looking straight at her weren't any kind of reassurance, either. She curled her fingers into the wrinkled cotton of his shirt and nodded, preparing herself for the news she didn't want to hear. "What's wrong? What's happened? Did you see a young woman here? Is she…" Lucy swallowed hard. "Is she okay?"

He eased his grip and straightened, raking one hand through his short muss of espresso-colored hair as he inhaled a deep breath. But he kept the other hand on her arm as if he suspected she might bolt again. "If you would come with me." He pulled her back into the hallway and closed the door to her condo behind them. "I need to ask you some questions."

Now he wanted to talk? After all those friendly overtures she'd made to her seriously hunky and completely-oblivious-to-a-lady-dropping-a-hint neighbor, tonight of all nights was when he wanted to have a private conversation with her? Somehow she doubted that he'd finally clued in on the crush she had on him. Preparing herself for a worst-case scenario, Lucy planted her feet before blithely following him into his condo. "Just tell me. Did you find a dead body in there? You told me you were a medical examiner during one of our elevator rides together when I first moved in. That's when I told you I was a social worker—that I've seen some pretty awful things, too. But my bodies weren't dead like yours. Just damaged in one way or another." Her mouth was rambling ahead of her brain. "I'm sorry. But you can tell me. Is this a crime scene? Is that why I can't go in there?" She touched the blood on his sleeve again. Although it was dry, its presence was disturbing. "Is this Diana's? Don't feel you have to spare my feelings. I've been sick out of my mind with worry all day. I just need a straight answer about what's happened. I can deal with anything—I'm good at that—as long as I know what I'm facing."

"You can deal with anything?" He angled his head to the side and his eyes narrowed, as if her plaintive assertion baffled him. Then he shook his head. "There is no dead body," he answered starkly. "I don't know who Diana is.

This blood is my grandfather's. He was shot yesterday afternoon at my sister's wedding."

"Shot? Oh, my God." Lucy's fingers danced over the ticklish hair of his forearm, wanting to act on her instinct to touch, to comfort, to fix the hurts of the world. "Is he okay? I mean, clearly he isn't. Getting shot is really bad. I'm sorry. Is he going to be all right?" His brusque answers explained the remnants of the James Bond getup, as well as the stains on what had once been a neatly ironed shirt. But what any of that had to do with the break-in or her or possibly Diana, she hadn't a clue. Lucy curled her fingers around the strap of her shoulder bag and retreated a step. "You don't need to worry about my problems. You should be with your family."

"Miss McKane." They were back to that now, hmm? "I'm sorry if the blood upset you—I haven't had time to change since coming home from the hospital." He scraped his palm over the dark stubble dotting his chin and jaw before sliding his fingers over his hair and literally scratching his head. "I can see I haven't explained myself very well. Your sympathy is appreciated but misplaced. My grandfather's condition is serious, but please, before you go off on another tangent, would you come inside? I do have a problem that concerns you specifically." He glanced toward the end of the hallway. "And I don't think we should have that conversation here."

She remembered the retired couple down the hall and nodded. "The Logans. I suppose it would be rude to wake them at this hour."

A man with a wounded grandfather, a gun and a badge, and an inexplicable sense of urgency could take precedence for a few minutes over her suspicions and the futile desperation that might even be unfounded. Lucy hadn't seen Diana Kozlow in months. Perhaps she'd read too much into the telephone message at the office this morning. She was probably chasing ghosts, thinking that Diana had really needed her. Roger Campbell hadn't needed her for anything more than sex and a punching board. The only reason her own mother had needed her was to ensure her own meal ticket. How many times did she have to repeat that codependent mistake?

Inhaling a deep breath, Lucy pulled off her left glove and cap and stuffed them into her pockets, too, as Niall opened the door for her to precede him. "So what concerns me specifically besides a busted front door..." She tried to smooth her staticky curls behind her ears. "Oh, hello."

At this late hour, she was surprised to see another man—a stockier version of Niall Watson, with a peppering of silver in his short dark hair—rising stiffly from a recliner as she stepped into the living room.

She extended her hand because she was that kind of friendly. "I'm Lucy McKane from across the hall. Sorry to visit so late, but Dr. Watson invited me…" The older man angled his body to face her, and she saw the blanket with tiny green and yellow animals draped over his arm. "You have a baby."

"Can't put anything past you," the tall man teased in a hushed voice, in deference to the tiny infant sleeping contentedly against his chest. "Thomas Watson." He easily cradled the child in one arm to shake her hand. "I raised three boys and a girl of my own, so I've had some practice. I'm Niall's father."

"I could tell by the family resemblance. Nice to meet you. You seem to be a natural." Lucy stepped closer to tuck the loose blanket back around the tiny child's head. The newborn's scent was a heady mix of gentle soap and something slightly more medicinal. A tightly guarded longing stirred inside her, and she wanted to brush aside the wisp of dark brown hair that fell across the infant's forehead. She wisely curled her fingers into her palm and smiled instead. "And this is…?"

Niall's crisp voice sounded behind her. "I was hoping you could tell us."

Lucy swiveled her head up to his as he moved in beside her. "I don't understand. Isn't the baby yours?" She glanced at Niall's father. He was older, yes, but by her quick assessment, still a virile man. "My apologies. The baby is yours."

"No, ma'am."

The older man grinned, but Niall looked anything but amused when he reached across her to adjust the blanket she'd tidied a moment earlier. "*I* broke into your apartment, Miss McKane."

"You? To steal twenty dollars? Why on earth would you do that?"

"I wasn't the first intruder. I found a screwdriver that had apparently been used to break into your place." He pulled a tiny gem from his pocket and held it up between his thumb and forefinger, twisting it until she could see the fracture in the clear red glass. "I believe this came off it."

"A screwdriver?" Lucy clutched at her purse strap, the bittersweet joy of seeing the baby momentarily forgotten. Diana *was* in trouble. "A pink one with glitter on the handle?"

He picked up a bag marked with numbers

and the scratch of his signature from the coffee table and folded the excess plastic out of the way so she could see the contents inside. "This one."

"Oh, my God." Lucy plucked the screwdriver from his open palm and turned it over in her hand. The room swayed at the instant recognition. Diana hadn't wanted jewelry or dolls for birthdays and Christmas. She'd been a tomboy and tough-kid wannabe from their first meeting. Diana had wanted a basketball and running shoes and a toolbox, although she'd seemed pleased with the bling on this particular set. Lucy blinked away the tears that scratched at her eyes and tilted her face to Niall's. "Where did you get this?"

"Is it yours?"

"Answer my question."

"Answer mine."

"Niall," Thomas gently chided.

A deep, resolute sigh expanded Niall Watson's chest before he propped his hands at his waist again in that vaguely superior stance that emphasized both his height and the width of his shoulders. If it wasn't for his glasses and the spiky muss of his hair that desperately needed a comb, she might have suspected he had an ego to go with all that intellect. "Apparently, someone jimmied the locks on your door several hours before I got home, and I suspect they used that tool to do it. I let myself in when I heard this child crying in distress. I thought, perhaps, you weren't being responsible—"

"With a child?" He thought…that she… Lucy didn't know whether to cry or smack him. "I would never. My job is to protect children."

"I know that." Her burst of defensive anger eased as he continued his account.

"But then I suspected that you might be in some kind of distress yourself. I entered the premises to make sure you were all right." He plucked the screwdriver from her fingers and returned it to the table along with the shattered bead and another bag that appeared to be holding the beginnings of the gray scarf she'd been knitting for a coworker. She could see now that the markings meant he'd labeled them all as evidence. "I found it on your kitchen counter beside the baby. I brought him here since there didn't seem to be anyone else watching him. We've given him food, clean clothes and a bath. Other than a nasty case of diaper rash, he seems to be healthy."

That explained the medicinal smell. "It's a boy?" She turned back to the older man cradling the sleeping infant. "He was in my apartment? All alone?"

"I believe that's what I've been saying." Niall Watson could sound as irritated with her as he wanted. He'd saved this child, and for that, she would be forever grateful.

Lucy pressed her fingers to her mouth to hold back the tears that wanted to fall. Tears that wouldn't do anyone any good. Diana's cryptic phone message that had sent Lucy on a wild hunt all over Kansas City finally made sense. "That's what she wanted to show me. I had no idea. The baby is what she wanted me to take care of. But why wouldn't she stay, too?"

"What are you talking about, Miss McKane?"

"I have a favor to ask, Lucy. I don't know who else to call. I need to show you something, and I need you to keep it safe."

"Why didn't she tell me?" Lucy whispered. She couldn't help but reach out to stroke her finger across the infant's cheek. His skin was as velvety soft as it looked, and she was instantly in love. "You precious little boy."

"Do you know who is responsible for this child?" Niall asked.

"Possibly." Lifting her gaze to Niall's father, Lucy held out her hands. "May I?"

"Of course."

Lucy sighed with a mixture of longing and regret as the baby's sweet weight filled her arms and settled against her. "He's so tiny. How old do you think he is?"

"I'd say a week. Two, tops," Niall answered from behind her. "Obviously, pediatrics isn't my area of expertise, but I know enough to handle the basics. I still think he needs to see a pediatric specialist to ensure a clean bill of health. Now what can you tell us about his parents?" Niall stepped aside as she circled the coffee table and sat on the edge of his sofa to hold the baby more securely. She heard a huff of what could be resignation a second before the cushion beside her sank with his weight. When she tumbled toward her tall neighbor at her shifting perch, his hands shot out to balance her shoulder and cradle her forearm that held the baby. "Easy. Don't let go of him."

"I couldn't."

Niall's hand remained beneath her arm, making sure of her hold on the infant. His chest pressed against Lucy's shoulder, and for a split second she was overcome by the normalcy of the family she'd never known and would never have. A mother, a father, a child they shared together. The yearning inside her was almost painful.

Blinking rapidly to dispel the impossible image of the brainy doctor cop and her creating a perfect little baby together, Lucy scooted away to break the contact between her and Niall Watson, although she could still feel that crazily addictive warmth he radiated. "What's his name?" she asked, craving the information as much as she needed to put space between her and her errant fantasies.

"He didn't come with an ID," Niall answered. "He didn't come with anything. Not even a fresh diaper. If you could answer at least some of my questions—"

"Son." The older Watson chided the tone in Niall's voice and offered her a smile. "I nicknamed him Tommy. But that's just a family name I was using so we could call him something besides 'little munchkin.' We were hoping you'd be able to fill in the blanks for us. But I take it you're not the mother."

His green eyes were kind, but Lucy still felt the sting of truth. "No. I...I can't have children of my own."

"I'm sorry. You seem like a natural with Tommy, too."

His kind words enabled her to smile back. "Thank you." But a glance up to the man seated beside her indicated that answers were the only thing that was going to soften that empirical focus zeroed in on her. He was this baby's champion, and nothing short of the entire truth was going to satisfy him. "I think... Tommy..." She stroked her fingertip over his tiny lips, and they instinctively moved to latch on, even though he was asleep. "I have no idea who the father is. But I think he belongs to my foster daughter, Diana Kozlow."

Niall's posture relaxed a fraction, although that stern focus remained. "The woman whose name you kept calling out."

Lucy nodded. "Technically, she's my former foster daughter. Diana was with me for six years until she aged out of the system. She's twenty now. We kept in touch for a year or so. But I lost contact with her after that. She changed her number, changed her job. I had no idea she'd gotten pregnant." She nodded toward the screwdriver on the coffee table. "I gave that to her in a tool set one Christmas. I guess she broke into my apartment to leave the baby with me. Probably took the twenty I had stashed in my knitting basket. She called me out of the blue yesterday—said she had some-*thing* she wanted to show me. I invited her for lunch today, but she never came. I tried calling the number she used, but the phone went straight to voice mail."

She rocked back and forth, ever so subtly, soothing the infant as he began to stir. "I went to my office to look up her most recent address and phone number to make sure I had it right— and discovered she'd left me a pretty disturbing message on my answering machine there. I've been out looking for her ever since. One of the neighbors at the last address where I knew her to live said Diana had a boyfriend move in with her about six months ago. She never knew his name, so that was a dead end. Shortly after that they moved to Carmody Street, she thought—"

"Carmody?" The elder Watson muttered a curse under his breath. "That's not a good part of town. You didn't go there to look for her by yourself, did you? At the police department, we call that part of town no-man's-land."

"I can believe it." The two men exchanged a grim look. "No one there recognized Diana, and they couldn't tell me the boyfriend's name, either. I wasn't sure where to look after that. How does a young woman just...disappear?" Lucy's thoughts drifted to all the morbid possibilities that had driven her to search for Diana. "Why wouldn't she keep Tommy with her?

Why wouldn't she stay at my place with him if she was in trouble?"

"*If* she's the mother," Niall cautioned. "We'd have to blood-type him and run DNA on both mother and son to be certain."

A DNA test couldn't tell Lucy what she already knew in her heart. "He looks like her—the shape of his face, the thick dark hair. What color are his eyes?"

Thomas shrugged. "You know, I don't remem—"

"Brown," Niall answered.

Lucy glanced up when he reached around her to tuck in the tiny fist that had pushed free of the blanket. She didn't mind Niall's unvarnished tone quite so much this time. He'd put his clinical eye for detail to work on doing whatever was best for this baby. "Diana has brown eyes."

Niall's startling blue gaze shifted to hers for a moment before he blinked and rose from the couch. He paced to the kitchen archway before turning to ask, "Did you save that message?"

Lucy nodded.

The two men exchanged a suspicious sort of glance before Thomas picked up a notepad and pen from the table beside the recliner. Niall adjusted his glasses on the bridge of his nose before splaying his fingers at his waist and facing her. "Maybe you'd better tell me more about your friend Diana. And why you thought she might be dead."

Chapter Three

Lucy added another round of quarters to the clothes dryer. "Oops. Sorry, munchkin."

She quickly apologized for the loud mechanical noise and leaned over the infant fastened into the carrier sitting on top of the dryer. But she needn't have worried. Tommy was still asleep, his tiny body swaying slightly with the jiggle of the dryer. She smiled, resisting the urge to kiss one of those round apple cheeks, lest she wake him again. He'd fussed and bellowed for nearly an hour upstairs before she remembered the advice she'd once heard from a coworker about tricks to help stubborn babies fall asleep and got the idea to bring Tommy and all his new clothes and supplies down to the basement laundry room to wash them.

Instead of disturbing him again, she opted to pull a blanket dotted with red, blue and yellow trucks from the basket of baby clothes she'd just unloaded and drape the cotton knit over him, securing him in a warm cocoon. Then she picked up the basket and set it on the neighboring dryer to start folding the rest of the light-colored sleepers and towels and undershirts. She was handling more than one problem here. She'd removed the noisy baby from Niall Watson's apartment so the enigmatic doctor could get some much-needed sleep. Since she had no chair to rock the baby in, she'd found the next best thing down here in the laundry room. And at this time of the morning, before the residents stirred to get ready for church or work, she'd found a quiet place for herself to think without being distracted by hunky neighbors with grabby hands and hard bodies, or caring for the needs of a newborn with too little sleep herself, or worrying about the unanswered calls and cryptic clues surrounding her foster daughter's disappearance.

When the second load of darker clothes was done in twenty minutes or so, she'd take Tommy back up to Niall Watson's apartment and sneak back in without waking him. Then she'd have another hour or two to curl up on his stiff leather couch and try not to notice how much the smell of it reminded her of the man himself. Crushes were terrible things when they were one-sided like this. Niall Watson, ME, was a good catch, according to her mother's standards—not that she credited Alberta McKane for giving her any useful set of values to judge a man by. But he was as dependable as he was curiously aloof, and that was a quality Lucy valued more than several framed degrees or the amount of money a man made. She vowed to be a good friend to her socially awkward neighbor, but she didn't have to torture her dreams with the vivid memory of his body flattened against hers as he pinned her to the wall. If he was a different man he'd have kissed her then. And chances are, she would have responded to that kiss with a purely female instinct.

But Niall Watson wasn't that man. He had a set of rules he lived by, an order of right and wrong he believed in. He wasn't a smooth talker. He wasn't much of a talker, period. But, awkward body contact aside, he treated her with respect. He put Tommy's and his family's needs above anything he and his hormones might feel. And that made him so much more attractive to her than anything her mother could have envisioned.

Stress, fatigue, the rhythmic sound of the

dryer and the warmth of the insulated laundry area were beginning to have the same hypnotic effect on Lucy as they did on Tommy. After several big blinks, her thoughts drifted and her hands came to rest in the pile of warm cotton garments. Her chin was dropping toward her chest when hushed voices entered her dreams. "Down here."

"Are you sure?"

"If her car's outside, but she's not at her place, then yes."

"This is a mistake."

"I just have to know—"

"Get out of here."

Lucy snapped her head up at the slam of a heavy door from somewhere above her. The muffle of words weren't inside her head. They were as real as the terse, angry exchange of voices bouncing off the concrete-block walls outside the laundry room. She touched the gentle rise and fall of Tommy's small chest, reassuring herself that he was safe, while she blinked the grogginess from her eyes and reoriented herself to the waking world. "Hello? Is someone there?"

"I know you're here," came a heavily accented voice. "You can't take what is mine."

Lucy thought she heard a bell. Someone getting off the elevator?

Or on it. "Move. Don't let him see you. Go!"

"Where is she?" the louder voice shouted. "You know what I want."

Lucy whirled around to the vicious argument, wondering if she was still half-asleep since she couldn't make out all the words.

"You stay away from her."

"You mind your own business."

Then she heard a grunt and a gasp plainly enough, before running feet stomped up the stairs.

"Diana?" Had she heard a woman's voice in the middle of all that? Or only dreamed it? Lucy fingered the phone in her jeans pocket. But the sounds of the argument were fading and she didn't want to panic the good doctor upstairs unnecessarily by waking him from a sound sleep.

"You stay away from her."

Oh, no. "Stay away from *me*?" Maybe Niall was already awake and dealing with some kind of trouble that she'd missed. What if someone *had* followed her to their apartment building and her neighbor had come downstairs to confront him? "Niall?"

If he got hurt, it would be her fault for getting him into this mess.

After ensuring that Tommy was still sleeping, Lucy ventured out into the hallway. It was empty now. Nothing but concrete walls and utility lights. Had the two parties she'd overheard arguing split up? The elevator was moving on the higher floors of the building, and whomever she'd heard run up the stairs had exited either out the side entrance to the parking lot or into the building's lobby. "Niall? Is that you? Who was—"

Lucy jumped at the loud thump against the steel door at the top of the stairs. Outside. They'd taken what could only be a fight, judging by the low-voiced curses and rattling door, out to the parking lot. "Niall!"

Lucy charged up the stairs, pulling her key card from her jeans and hurrying out the door to the harsh sounds of a revving engine and tires squealing to find traction along the pavement. She saw the silhouette of a man racing between the cars. "Niall? Hey! Don't hurt him!"

She glanced toward the front entrance as one of the glass doors swung open. Was help coming? Or more trouble? She should call 911. She reached for her phone.

But when she saw the running figure lurch

as if some invisible force had jerked him back a step, she sprinted forward to help. "Stop!"

There were two men trading blows out there. One had ambushed the other.

"Lucy!" The warning barely registered as her feet hit the pavement. She glimpsed the man hitting the ground a split second before a pair of headlights flashed on their high beams and blinded her.

Forced to turn away, she stumbled back a step. She thought she heard another car door open. She knew she heard the terrible sound of a transmission grinding too quickly through its gears. The headlights grew bigger, like a nocturnal predator bearing down on her. The lights filled up her vision. The roar of the engine deafened her. The heat of the powerful car distorted the chill of the early February morning.

"Lucy!"

Two arms slammed around her body and lifted her out of harm's way. She hit the hard earth with a jolt and tumbled, rolling two or three times until she wound up flat on her back with Niall Watson's long body pinning her to the ground.

She noted the flash of a silver sports car speeding past, bouncing over the curb into the street and disappearing into the night before the strong thigh pressed between her legs and the muscled chest crushing her breasts and the hot gasps of Niall's deep breaths against her neck even registered. "I knew that car was following me…" Lucy's triumphant words trailed away in a painful gurgle as the pain of that tackle bloomed through her chest. "Oh, man. That hurts."

"Not as much as getting mowed down by that Camaro would have." She flattened her palms against his shoulders and tried to push, but he only rose up onto his elbows on either side of her, leaving their hips locked together. He glared down at her through those dark frames. "What were you thinking? Didn't you see him driving right at you?"

"I thought you were hurt." She sucked in a deeper breath and found more voice as the ache in her lungs eased. "There was a fight outside the laundry room. He knocked the other man down. I thought it was you."

"It wasn't."

"Duh." Her breath returned in shallow gasps. "What are you doing here, anyway?"

"Saving you, apparently."

"You're supposed to be asleep."

"You're supposed to be in my apartment."

Lucy was blatantly aware of cold ground and

damp clothes and the black KCPD T-shirt that left little of that sleekly muscled torso to her imagination now. But Niall flattened himself right back on top of her when another vehicle engine roared to life in the parking lot. She found herself flat on her back a second time, pinned beneath Niall's body as the second car raced past.

Only after it turned into the street and sped away after the silver Camaro did Niall raise his head again. "Do you recognize that vehicle, too?"

Lucy shook her head. She hadn't even gotten a look at it. A fat lot of help she was. As her body warmed in places it shouldn't, Lucy gave him another push. "You can get off me now."

Without even so much as a *sorry for invading your personal space and making your brain short-circuit again*, Niall rolled to his feet and extended a hand to help her stand up beside him. While she brushed at the mud on her knees and bottom, he bent down to pick up her key card and phone and pressed them into her hands. "Are you hurt?"

"No."

Despite her answer, he turned her hands over and inspected the muddy smear on her elbow.

"What are you doing out here at this time of the blessed a.m.?"

Lucy plucked away the dead bits of grass that clung to the scruff of his beard and hair. "Are *you* hurt?"

"Lucy," he prompted, dismissing her concern. "Give me an answer."

She pulled away and shrugged, wondering how long she was going to feel that stiff catch in her chest, and how much of it had to do with hitting the ground so hard and how much had to do with learning Niall's shape in a far-too-intimate way. "I heard voices. Someone was fighting on the basement stairs, and they ran out. One of them got on the elevator, maybe. I was half-asleep."

"Where's the baby?"

"Tommy." Her blood chilling at what a doofus she was turning out to be at this whole instant-motherhood thing, Lucy ran back to the side exit. She slid her key card into the lock and pulled the door open.

Niall was right behind her. "I woke up, and you and Tommy were gone." That explained the bare feet and pseudo pajamas he was wearing. "I saw the sacks with all his clothes had disappeared, too. When you weren't in your apartment, either, I came down to look for you.

Then I heard the engine outside. For a second I thought—"

"What? That I'd run off and taken the baby?" She hurried down the steps. Niall followed right behind her. "I would never do that. You're just as important to him as I am." The door to the laundry room had closed, and she quickly accessed it with her key card while Niall glanced up at the numbers lighting up on the elevator behind them. But he caught the door and followed her in as she hurried to the baby carrier still rocking on top of the clothes dryer. Her breath rushed out with relief when she saw those sweet brown eyes tracking their movement across the room. "Thank goodness. He's fine. He was being so fussy. I fed him and changed him and still couldn't get him to stop crying, and you said you hadn't slept in forty-eight hours. So I remembered a trick that one of the older women in my office said worked for her kids when they wouldn't sleep. Besides, all these new things need to be washed before he can wear them."

"You left him here alone?"

"I must have dozed off myself until I heard the argument out in the hallway." Lucy un-hooked the straps on the carrier and reached for Tommy. "There you are, sweetie. See? He's fine. Wide-awake again, hmm—"

"Wait." Niall's hand on her arm startled her. "Don't touch him."

She glanced up to the narrow-eyed scrutiny behind his glasses. "What's wrong?"

"How long were you gone?"

"I don't know. A few minutes, maybe..." And then she zeroed in on what had put Niall on alert. There was a lipstick mark on Tommy's forehead. Without asking, the scientist beside her captured Lucy's chin and tilted it up to run his thumb over her mouth with a friction that tingled across her lips and made her tremble from head to toe.

Despite her body's traitorous response to his firm touch, it wasn't meant to be a caress. Niall released her and held the tip of his thumb beside the mark on Tommy's forehead. The gloss she wore was rosy pink. The color on Tommy's skin was a tannish coral.

"Oh, my God." She *had* heard a woman's voice earlier. Another woman had been in here when Tommy was alone. That whole fight must have been a distraction—a way to get Lucy to leave while another woman sneaked into the laundry room. She'd kissed the baby while Lucy had been chasing shadows and dodging cars.

"Someone was here," Niall pronounced.

Not someone.

"Diana." Lucy quickly glanced around, realizing what she should have seen when she'd unhooked Tommy from his carrier. The clean, warm blanket she'd covered him with was missing. "She took the blanket I put over him. She was right here."

And now the young woman was gone.

Again.

Chapter Four

Niall clipped his badge onto the belt of his jeans, debated about leaving his gun locked inside its metal box, then decided to strap it on. If Diana Kozlow was in serious trouble, as Lucy claimed—and the twenty-year-old hadn't simply punked out on the responsibility and expense of caring for a baby—then he'd do well to be prepared for any contingency that could come back to harm Tommy or Lucy.

It wasn't just his civic-minded sense of duty that prompted him to take a proactive role in guarding the security of his building and neighbors—too many unanswered questions surrounding the baby still nagged at him. Before he'd left, Thomas Watson had suggested Niall keep an eye open for further suspicious activity around the building. Certainly, alleged fights and a silver Camaro nearly running down Lucy—either intentionally or as collateral damage in a speedy getaway from the second driver—qualified as suspicious.

He couldn't tell yet if that woman was simply a magnet for trouble or if she was truly embroiled in a legitimate missing-person case. Niall trusted his dad's gut warning him that something felt seriously wrong here as much as he trusted his own assessment of the clues surrounding Tommy, the violation of Lucy's apartment and those two near misses in the parking lot last night. The break-in had been an act of desperation, not planning. The mark of lipstick on Tommy's forehead that didn't match Lucy's dark pink color indicated a kiss. From a guilt-ridden mother reluctant to say goodbye to a baby she couldn't take care of on her own? Or a frightened young woman who saw no other option to keep her son safe than to abandon him to her most trusted friend?

But safe from what? Or whom?

If he hadn't been reliving the nightmare of the shooting at his sister's wedding and woken himself up to clear his head, he wouldn't have discovered Lucy and Tommy missing from his living room. He wouldn't have gone looking for them and seen his pretty neighbor blinded by the car barreling toward her. He wouldn't have known that gut-wrenching sense of helpless inadequacy knowing that someone out there was a step ahead of him, luckier—if not smarter—than he was when it came to taking care of an impulsive woman and an innocent child.

And Niall needed to be able to take care of Lucy and Tommy. He hadn't spotted the shooter soon enough. He hadn't prevented his grandfather from stroking out. And unless a dead body showed up on his autopsy table, there wasn't a damn thing he could do to help his family figure out who had targeted Seamus in the first place. But watching over Lucy and Tommy was something he could do. Helping them find Diana Kozlow and the other answers they needed was the challenge that would keep him busy and his mind occupied. Helping them was the worthwhile difference he *could* make.

Besides, there was something about a tiny baby who quieted at the sound of his voice or the touch of his hand that awakened something so alien inside Niall that he'd almost forgotten the words his mother had once spoken to him as a child. He'd been bewailing going to a new school after moving across Kansas City. Athletic Duff and outgoing Keir had made new friends easily enough. But gangly, bookish Niall, who'd inherited his mother's shy genes, had spent the first few weeks of fourth grade feeling utterly alone. She'd climbed up into the tree house where he'd been hiding out to share a hug and some loving wisdom. *"There are certain people in this world, Niall, that we are destined to have a special connection to. You don't need a lot of friends. Just one or two who understand you. Who'll have your back. Who need you to be their friend, too."*

Perhaps she'd been referring to his brothers and sister sharing that kind of closeness with him. But the very next day, he'd met another new student on the playground, and the two of them had become good friends who'd gone through middle school and high school together. Although they'd taken separate college and career paths, he and Jack Riggins still kept in touch.

The moment he'd picked up Tommy, Niall had felt a similar, irrational connection being made. Tommy liked him. Tommy needed him to be his friend. Whether as a doctor or rescuer or simply as an authoritative presence to quiet his tears, Niall Watson intended to be there for Tommy Kozlow—or whatever the little boy's name turned out to be.

Tommy's real identity was only one of several questions Niall intended to find answers to today. As soon as he checked in with his grandfather at the hospital and reported any medical updates to his family, he wanted to assess Diana Kozlow's fitness as a parent, determine whether the danger Lucy suspected was genuine and track down the missing mother. And, if Diana wouldn't share the father's name, or a birth certificate couldn't be found, Niall planned to work out the legalities between guardianship and what was in the child's best interest and obtain permission to draw some of Tommy's blood to run his DNA to locate the boy's father. Lucy had already put the paperwork into motion to secure temporary foster placement of the baby with her. Her permission would be enough to run Tommy's DNA and give him his real name, so there was that conversation on his agenda today, as well.

That should be plenty to keep him busy until he reported back to work at the lab tonight.

Prepared with a plan for the next several hours, Niall ran a comb through his damp hair and picked up his mug of cold decaf off the dresser before heading out into the living room, where he'd left Lucy and Tommy sleeping a couple hours earlier.

His structured day quickly hit its first glitch when he saw that the lamp beside the sofa was on and his guests were both wide-awake. Niall stopped, his eyes narrowing on the crown of Lucy McKane's dark curls as she leaned over the baby in her lap. Nerve endings in his chest and thighs awakened with a mysterious sense memory, recalling the impression of soft curves pressing against his harder angles during that tussle in the hallway and that tumble across the grass last night. He was equally fascinated by her hands. Royal blue yarn dangled from her fingers as she deftly twisted knots onto the slender pair of knitting needles she worked. The glossy kinks of her hair bobbed against her shoulders and over the curves of the mud-stained sweater she still wore as she played peekaboo with Tommy.

She knit several stitches, then clutched her work to her chest and teased Tommy with an "I see you" that made his little fists pump with delight. The baby gurgled and cooed when she brushed his nose and shook her hair against his fingers. Then he calmed when she went back to knitting and obscured her face again.

Niall studied the interchange twice before Lucy looked up and smiled. "You know, you can stare at the details for so long that you miss the bigger picture."

He hadn't missed a thing. Abandoned baby.

A woman who was proving more intriguing to study than she should be, making herself at home on his couch. Apparently, despite his insistence that her apartment wouldn't be safe for her and Tommy until maintenance could come and replace her locks, she'd sneaked inside a second time. "Excuse me?"

Lucy cupped the half-formed cap she'd been knitting over Tommy's head before tying it off and pointing to the wet bar. "Diaper. You don't smell that? Our little friend here has been very busy since I gave him his last bottle. I left the changing pad over there and didn't want to risk moving him in case he made a mess on your nice leather sofa. Your place isn't exactly baby-proofed."

Niall glanced at the stockpile of supplies his father had brought over and crossed the room to get the things she needed. "The sofa has no sentimental value. It can be cleaned. You should have called me if you needed help with the baby."

"You were in the shower."

He returned to the couch, nodding toward the basket of knitting supplies she'd retrieved from her apartment. "Longer than I thought, apparently. You went back to your place. After that incident in the laundry room last night, I thought we'd agreed that you'd stay put."

"No. You suggested it. I promised to be careful," she clarified. "Tommy was sound asleep on the pallet we made for him, so I figured it'd be fine to go across the hall to gather up my knitting. I like to keep my hands busy. Especially when there's a lot on my mind." She thanked him for the supplies and set up a changing station beside her before moving Tommy onto the pad and dropping down to her knees in front of the couch. "I didn't want to wake you because, well, I already woke you once, and I could tell you needed to sleep." She turned her face up to his and winked. "You still look tired, if you ask me."

"I didn't." Niall picked up the soiled diaper and carried it to the kitchen trash. "I'm used to keeping odd hours. I'm fine."

"No, you're not," she insisted, strapping a fresh diaper into place. "How can it be with everything you've had to deal with in the past forty-eight hours or so? I imagine your job is pretty stressful, but I'm guessing your weekends don't always include a wedding, your grandfather going into the hospital, and the wacky neighbor lady and a baby taking refuge in your living room."

Wacky? His analysis of Lucy McKane had included terms like *caring, vibrant, sensual*. Although *garrulous, stubborn* and *unpredictable* were certainly apt descriptors, too.

Niall shook his head, puzzled by how easily his thoughts seemed to derail around this woman. Perhaps the shower and shave hadn't revived him as much as he'd hoped and he needed to switch to caffeinated coffee to unfog his brain. The important point here was that she'd taken another unnecessary risk, negating the whole purpose of him insisting she and Tommy take refuge in his apartment. He picked up a new outfit from the laundry she'd folded and carried it to the couch. "What if the intruders had come back?"

"You mean Diana? Then I would have brought her here and helped her, too."

She was making assumptions that couldn't yet be proved. "What if Diana had nothing to do with breaking into your apartment? What if hers wasn't the woman's voice you heard last night?"

"Who else would kiss—"

"What if someone took advantage of her connection to you, borrowed her toolbox and broke in to surrender a baby without any legal hassles?"

"And knew where I hid some extra cash?"

Fine. If Lucy was so certain Tommy was Diana's son, he had a reasonable argument for that, too. "What if the threat that prompted Diana to abandon Tommy in the first place followed her to your apartment? What if those men you heard last night had come back for you? To finish something they'd started? You could have been seriously hurt."

Her fingers stopped. Everything about her seemed to pause for a split second before Lucy shook her head, spilling her hair over the neckline of her sweater. As quickly as she'd frozen, she went right back to changing the baby, lifting Tommy to position the new sleeper beneath his back. "I appreciate your concern. But I was only gone a few minutes—long enough to clean up the cookie dough spoiling in the kitchen and gather up my knitting. If I'd sensed anything was wrong, I would have come straight back. Nothing happened."

"This time." Niall adjusted his glasses, averting both his gaze and the unexpected flare of curiosity about her reaction to the suggestion that she, and not Tommy or Diana, was the one in danger. Was it wrong of him to want to push her to reveal just what had caused her to hesitate like that? And he wondered if she knew she had a long tendril of hair caught in the nubby tweed of her sweater. He could easily reach down and free the strand for her. When he'd knocked her out of the way of that speeding car last night, he'd inadvertently discovered that her hair was as silky as it looked. That the ends were cool to the touch and the length of it was as strongly resilient as the woman herself. His fingers itched to tangle in those curly locks again, to re-create the chance touch and confirm his observations. Niall blinked away the thought. *That* wasn't on the agenda for today. She was changing Tommy's diaper, for pity's sake, not seducing him. "Lucy, I need to know that you're taking this seriously. I believe Tommy was in grave danger yesterday. That means you could be, too. I need you to be able to take care of him so that I can conduct my investigation."

"So that we can conduct *our* investigation," she corrected, as if he had misspoken. Lifting Tommy into her arms, she stood, cradling the infant against her chest and gazing down into his attentive brown eyes. "I appreciate more than you know that you and your father promised to help me find Diana and reunite her with her son. I'm grateful that you offered to let us stay with you until maintenance can replace the locks on my door. I wouldn't have felt safe there."

"You weren't. You still aren't."

She looked up at him then. "I'm grateful that you probably saved me from my own impulsiveness last night. But don't think for one moment that I don't know how serious this situation is. If Tommy and I are in danger, then Diana must be facing something worse. If she has anything to do with those men I heard arguing last night, then I know she is. I know her better than anyone. At least, I used to. You need my help."

"And if I don't accept it, you'll go off searching the city for her on your own again, won't you."

Lucy's expression brightened with a wry smile. "Now *that* is an accurate conclusion, Dr. Watson."

Not understanding the giggle that followed, Niall simply nodded, conceding the wisdom of having someone with inside information on Diana Kozlow to guide his investigation so he could either confirm or rule out Lucy's belief that Tommy was her foster daughter's baby. It pleased him, too, to know that Lucy would have temporary custody of Tommy as a foster parent, keeping the little boy close by so that

Niall could keep watch over him, too. "So we agree to work as a team. For Tommy's sake."

"For Tommy's sake." She took a step closer, and Niall inhaled the scents of baby powder and something slightly more exotic that didn't have anything to do with the infant she was pushing into his arms. "Since I've convinced you that we're on the same side now, would you feel comfortable watching him for about ten minutes? That's all the time I'll need to freshen up and change so we're ready to go." Her fingers caught for a moment between Tommy and the placket of his shirt, and even through the pressed cotton, Niall's stomach muscles clenched at the imprint of her knuckles brushing against his skin. But she pulled away to drape a burp rag over his shoulder, apparently unaware of his physiological reactions to her touch and scent. "You still want to drive us to my office to pick up a bassinet and some other supplies?" she asked, gathering up her boots and purse and sweater coat.

"*I'm* the one with a car seat, so yes, I'm driving." Niall shook off his weary brain's inability to focus and shifted Tommy to one arm, catching the door as she stepped into the hallway. "I want to listen to that message from your foster daughter, too, before I bring you back here."

He entered her living room right behind her, frowning at how easy it had been for her to push open the damaged door. He plowed into her before realizing she had stopped. "What are you doing?"

Her hands went straight to Tommy, even as she stumbled back a step. "What are *you* doing?" she asked. She released her grip once she seemed assured that there was no chance of him dropping the baby.

Niall looked over the top of her head to scan the empty, seemingly undisturbed living room. "I want to check your apartment before allowing you to remain here for any length of time on your own."

She nodded her understanding of his intention and crossed to a lamp to flip it on and fill the room with light. She opened the powder-room door so he could see it was clear, as well. "Your dad said we have to wait twenty-four hours to file an official missing-person case on Diana with KCPD. I'm glad you both agreed that we could start looking for answers sooner."

He followed her to the kitchen and saw that, other than the dishes she'd washed, it, too, showed no signs of the intruder returning.

"Tommy needs his mother. If we can locate her and reunite them—"

"And make sure she's okay—"

"—and ensure she's competent enough and able to care for him—"

"Competent?" Lucy planted her feet, and Niall nearly knocked her flying again. But she put up a hand with a huff of exasperation, and it was Niall who retreated a step this time. "Diana would never abandon Tommy unless something was terribly wrong and she thought it was for the best. People like her and me, we have issues about family. When you've never had one, once you get one…you protect it with everything you have in you. I have to believe that, whatever's wrong, she left Tommy here in order to protect him."

"Then why come back for him? If that was her in the laundry room last night."

"Her instinct may be to protect him, but giving up the family you love, especially your brand-new child…I can't imagine how hard that would be. I don't know if I could be strong enough to say goodbye to this little one." Lucy reached out to stroke Tommy's hair as if she'd already convinced herself that Tommy was her family now. A conclusion founded purely on emotions, no doubt.

Niall—and the law in the state of Missouri—required more incontrovertible proof. "You told Dad your mother was still alive when he was taking down your personal history, asking about other people Diana might have contacted. You have family."

"Trust me, I don't. Family are people who love you unconditionally. People you can trust and rely on. The man who sired me left before I was ever born, and my mother and I have been estranged since I emancipated myself at seventeen. She's not a part of my life anymore. She never will be again."

"What happened?"

Lucy curled her fingers into her hand and turned down the hallway. "Any number of things from not always having a place to live to the revolving door of men she *did* try to make a home with. But my breaking point was when we had a difference of opinion about my boyfriend." Although she laughed, Niall was certain there was no humor in that wry sound. "It's not what you think. I wasn't some kind of teenage rebel wanting to date a bad boy. In fact, she did everything she could to encourage me to keep the guy I was trying to get away from."

"Get away from?" Niall wondered at the fist of suspicion that hit him as squarely as discovering a clue on his autopsy table. "Why? What did he do to you?"

When she faced him this time, her eyes had dulled to a mossy shade of green. "Funny. My mother was more upset about what I'd done to him." Niall waited for her to elaborate. Lucy didn't disappoint. "Roger was Falls City's golden boy—you know how it is in a small town—the high school's star quarterback, Daddy runs the manufacturing plant that employs most of the town. But Roger and I weren't a good fit."

"How so?"

"No question is too personal for you, is it?" Her typically direct gaze dropped to the middle button of his shirt. Instead of giving an immediate answer, Lucy pulled a towel from the linen closet and hugged it to her chest before turning and tilting her gaze back up to his. "All that mattered to my mother was that Roger was rich. He was going to take over the family business one day. And if he was interested in me, then no matter how awful that relationship was I needed to suck it up and…" She paused midsentence to lean in and press a kiss to Tommy's temple as the baby dozed in his arms. Niall felt that wistful caress as though her mouth had made the connection against his own skin. Before he could question his empathetic response, Lucy shook her head and headed into the bathroom to set the towel on the edge of the sink. "I realized I was just a tool for her. It was easier than I expected to leave her and move to Kansas City. I've been on my own ever since. With the exception of Diana, of course. There's no blood between us, but she's family more than my mother ever was."

Niall considered the vehemence of her statement, detecting not one trace of melancholy or regret as he followed her into the small room. "And Roger?"

Her slender shoulders sagged briefly before she straightened. "Testified against him. Sent him to prison instead of college."

"For what?"

Her eyes met his in the mirror. "No more questions right now, okay?"

Niall needed a last name. He intended to follow up on this Roger lowlife and decide if he had anything to do with Tommy's abandonment—or even if he could be the child's father. But he'd follow up on a different tack until Lucy opened up again. "I'd give anything to see my mother again."

"I have a feeling you were raised very differently than I was. Your father is funny and kind, and I believe he truly cares about Tommy and Diana, and maybe even me. The way he told me all about your brothers and sister and his dad?" She turned, sitting her hip back on the counter of the sink. She was smiling again, and for some reason, seeing the soft curve of her lips seemed to take some of the edge off the concern that wasn't entirely professional. "I could tell that Thomas is really proud of each of you. And clearly, he loves you and supports you. It's not every son or daughter who has a parent who drops everything in the middle of the night to do some emergency shopping for them. Even when you're a grown-up. You're lucky."

Niall concurred. "I know."

A genuine laugh echoed off the tile walls. "You are one of a kind, Doctor. You see everything in black-and-white, don't you? Sometimes I envy your ability to ignore your emotions."

Funny, he'd been thinking he'd better understand his reactions to her and that mysterious Roger devil he'd never met if he could turn off the emotional responses she seemed to evoke in him and take the time to analyze whether it was fatigue, the sense of duty he was raised with—or the fact he hadn't interacted this closely with a woman on a personal basis since some time back in med school—that was clouding his perceptions.

Lucy curled her finger into Tommy's tiny hand and tucked it in beside Niall's arm. "I'm sorry about your mother. If a man like your dad loved her, I'm sure she was someone special."

"She was."

"Diana never met my mother. I wouldn't let Alberta McKane get close to anyone I cared about. The woman is toxic." A chilly palm print marked Niall's shoulder as she pushed him out the door into the hallway. "Now go. I still need ten minutes."

Lucy was dressed in jeans and a Kansas City Royals sweatshirt and was ready to go in nine. Since she was motivated to work and Tommy was content to watch them do so, it made sense to set aside his curiosity about Lucy McKane's past and focus on the very present problem of locating Diana Kozlow and identifying Tommy's birth parents and possibly the man who had nearly run down Lucy with his fancy car.

Niall loaded a bassinet and stroller into the back of his SUV while Lucy packed a new diaper bag with items they'd picked up en route to her office at Family Services. They stopped to feed Tommy four more ounces of formula before he fell asleep on Lucy's shoulder. Only then did the dark-haired woman with the riot of silky curls tumbling over her shoulders sit down at the pod of four desks surrounding a power pole and play the messages on her answering machine.

After the first beep, a man's voice, possibly slurred by alcohol, came on the line. *"Hey, Luce, it's me. I know I screwed up. I need to see you, sweet thing. I just want to apologize. Make things right between us. Please don't—"*

Lucy's cheeks reddened and she punched the button, cutting off the rest of the drawling message. "Ignore him."

"Is that a client?"

He wondered if she would ever tell him a lie to escape answering one of his questions. "Roger Campbell. High school ex. Somehow he's gotten my work number. I guess it's not tricky. We're a state institution listed in the phone book. He must have asked the main desk to transfer his call to my extension."

"Could he have your personal information, too? Does he know where you live? If you testified against him—"

She shook off his questions and pulled up the next message on the machine. Not a lie. But not an answer, either. "Here's the recording I want you to listen to."

"Lucy? It's Diana. I won't be able to make it for lunch. I know that doesn't makes sense after calling you yesterday when I hadn't called you at all for a while and I changed my number and...I'm sorry. I have so much to tell you, but...there's really no time right now." The younger woman's voice was already hurried and breathless, but now it dropped to such a soft whisper that Niall sat on the edge of the desk and leaned in to hear it over the muted mechanical noises grinding in the background. *"Something's come up and I have to take care of it. I thought I could handle it myself, but... I have a favor to ask, and I don't know who else to call. I need to give you something, and I need you to keep it safe while I..."* There was a sniffle and a hushed gasp. Diana was crying. Niall looked across the desk to discover Lucy's eyes tearing up, as well. *"We're family, right? I need you to have my back even though I don't deserve it. I really made a mess this time. But I can fix it...I have to fix it..."*

There was another sob, and Lucy's fingers began a slow massage up and down Tommy's back. A quick gasp ended the weeping on the answering machine. The muffled shout of someone calling through a door or wall triggered the sound of quick footsteps. *"I have to go. I'll get there as soon as I can, but I can't stay. I'll explain everything when there's more time. You're the only one I can count on. Please."* Then, in a louder voice, Diana added, *"I'm here. Yes, I'm alone. Who would I be talking to? Just hold your—"*

He heard a muffled commotion at the end of the message, as if Diana had been hiding the phone in her purse or pocket before she finished disconnecting the call. Even with Niall's limited imagination, it was impossible to miss the distinct sounds of the young woman's distress.

Niall had never seen the stoic expression lining Lucy's face before as she pressed a button to save the message. "I waited at my apartment for her to bring me this mysterious *thing*, and when she didn't show up, I went looking for her. Of course, I didn't know where to go. I went to the hair salon where she used to work, but they said she hadn't been there in ages. I tried her old apartment. The boyfriend I knew said she'd moved out months earlier. Then I went to the place on Carmody Street. I hit a dead end. How does a twenty-year-old drop out of sight like that?"

"And you tried the cell phone number she called you from? You said her voice mail was completely full?"

Lucy nodded. "I'm right to be worried, aren't I? Tommy is the *something* she wanted me to keep safe. And it sounded to me as if she didn't want anyone on her end of the conversation to listen in." When Lucy rolled the chair away from her desk and stood, Niall did the same. "I didn't recognize the other voice, but it sounded like a man, don't you think? I couldn't make out what he was saying, though. Just like that argument last night."

"Because the man wasn't speaking English." Niall had been listening to more than just the recorded words. "Does she know a foreign language? Would she have understood the man?"

"She took Spanish in high school. That wasn't Spanish. I know enough of that to at least identify it."

It would require a bit of research, but Niall was thinking the words had been something more Russian or Germanic. They'd been angry words. And Diana Kozlow had definitely been afraid. Even though he expected it to be archived, he wanted to read through Diana's Family Services file to see if there was any friend or reference or job connection that might link her to a man with a foreign accent.

After staring at him expectantly for a few moments, Lucy swiped away her tears and made efficient work of strapping Tommy into his carrier and covering him with a blanket. She replaced the cap on his bottle and folded the burp rag to tuck into the diaper bag. "What are you thinking, Niall?"

Although Diana had been vague in her request and had never mentioned a baby or Tommy's real name, he could see that Lucy believed the younger woman and this child had been in terrible danger. For the moment, Niall agreed. Certainly, Carmody Street was no place for a young woman with a baby to take refuge. He reached out and stopped Lucy's hand from zipping the bag shut. "You can't go back to the apartment by yourself until we know more." And he damn sure didn't want her there by herself until he'd run a background check on Roger Campbell. "I need to analyze that recording at the crime lab. I have a friend who's a sound engineer there who owes me a favor. I'll call him, and we'll go there after the hospital."

Her gaze darted up to meet his, and he felt her skin warming beneath his touch before she turned her hand to squeeze his fingers then pull away to finish packing. "But we've already been too much of an imposition. You need to go by Saint Luke's to visit your grandfather and spend time with your family. I've already kept you from them longer than you planned this morning. I can grab the car seat and call a cab so you don't even have to drive us. Tommy and I will be fine—as long as you don't mind us staying in your apartment. Maintenance said there was a chance they could get someone to see to my locks today."

"And they also said it could be Monday morning." No. Tommy needed Dr. Niall Watson of the KCPD crime lab to be his friend right now. And no matter how independent she claimed to be, Lucy needed a friend, too. Right now that friend was going to be him. Niall shrugged into his black KCPD jacket and picked up the sweater coat she'd draped over the back of her chair. "I work quickly and methodically, Lucy. I will find the answers you and Tommy need. But I can't do that when I'm not able to focus. And having half the city between you and me when we don't know what all this means or if you and Tommy are in any kind of danger—"

"Are you saying I'm a distraction?"

Nothing but. Confused about whether that was some type of flirtatious remark or whether she was simply seeking clarification, Niall chose not to answer. Instead, he handed her the sweater and picked up Tommy in his carrier. "Get his things and let's go."

Chapter Five

"I'm so sorry to hear about your foster daughter. If Niall says he'll find her, he will. I've never known that boy not to solve a puzzle. Don't give up hope."

"I won't." Lucy tried to imagine how different her life might have been if she'd had Millie Leighter for a grandmother or a sweet spinster aunt or even just a friend growing up in Falls City. With Tommy charmingly blowing bubbles and taking an instant liking to the plump silver-haired woman, too, Lucy had spent the last hour in the fifth-floor lobby waiting area at Saint Luke's Hospital getting to know the fellow knitter along with a little Watson family history.

Millie had been hired by Thomas Watson when Niall had barely been a teenager, after the murder of Mary Watson. Seamus had come to live with the family then, too, to help give the stunned, grieving children and their father a sense of normalcy and security. By turns touched and then genuinely amused, Lucy listened to Millie's stories about Duff's penchant for making trips to the emergency room, Niall's awkward shyness, Keir's vivid imagination and Olivia's ability to keep the brothers who were twice her size in line. But all the while Lucy kept remembering flashes of her own childhood and teen years, when her mother had sent her out to beg for coins so they could buy dinner. Or later, when her mother would send her to the park to play to keep her away from the trailer they sometimes lived in while Alberta slept with the crooked local sheriff to stave off getting arrested for shoplifting. Millie's humorous rendition of the New Year's celebration when Seamus had reheated a bunch of leftover pizza and she'd had to come home from her vacation to take care of an entire family stuck in the bathroom with food poisoning made Lucy laugh at the miserable story. But she couldn't help but feel the sting of useless jealousy.

She had no such loving anecdotes to share about growing up, no dear friend she'd been able to call when she really needed someone.

She'd gotten herself to the hospital that night Roger Campbell had beaten her so badly. And the only reason her mother had come to visit her after the emergency surgery that had nearly gutted her was to advise her to accept Roger's apology and take him back.

It was almost impossible for her to imagine being part of a family as close and supportive as Niall's, despite the tragedies the Watsons had faced. But she could very well imagine her being a friend to a generous woman like Millie Leighter.

"Oh, my. Little Tommy's dropped off again." Millie glanced up as the elevator dinged across from the carpeted waiting area. An orderly rolled a noisy cart of lunch trays into the hallway, trading a greeting with the clerk at the floor's main desk. "I'm surprised all this hustle and bustle hasn't kept him awake."

Lucy smiled at the tiny bundle of baby nestled against Millie's chest. "Are you getting tired of holding him?"

"Not on your life."

"He's content. I'm sure he enjoyed your stories as much as I did."

Millie's cheeks warmed with a blush. "Pish-posh. You're a dear for letting me rattle on so."

"It fills the time while we're waiting to hear

about Seamus. I know I can talk ninety miles a minute when I'm nervous or worried about something."

"I don't believe that." The older woman smiled. "You're trapped here with me because Niall didn't leave you a way to get home. But I thank you for listening." Millie's smile faded. "I live in a house with police officers, and I know their work is dangerous. I've been through a lot with them—kept the ship running through good times and tough ones, so to speak. But I've never been in the middle of a shooting myself, and I'm not handling this very well. I'll never forget the awful sound of all those guns firing, and the screams, and…watching Seamus crumple to the floor like that. There was so much blood. I thought…I was certain…"

Lucy reached across the gap between their chairs to comfort the other woman. "I can't imagine what it must have been like to be there."

Millie sniffled away the tears that threatened to spill over. She patted Lucy's hand before pulling up the cotton blanket Tommy was swaddled in to shield his face from the hospital's bright lights. "New life like this is always the best antidote for a horrific experience like that. And so is friendly conversation. Now why don't you tell me something about you. What were you like as a little girl?"

Not Lucy's favorite topic of conversation. She sat back in the cushioned chair, running through the short list of memories she was willing to share. "Well…I had a next-door neighbor who taught me how to knit when I was in the fourth grade. I made everybody I knew a pot holder for Christmas that year. They got scarves the year after that."

"And now you're creating intricate patterns like those beautiful socks you're wearing. The curved needles give me fits. I invariably drop a stitch. If you have any hints—" A door opened down the hallway and Lucy turned as the older woman straightened in her seat to look across the carpeted waiting area. "There are Thomas and the boys. I wonder if they have any news."

Duff came out of the room first. "That guy disappeared like a freakin' magician. One minute I'm running after him on the roof, and then poof—he jumps onto the next building and he's gone."

Keir Watson followed. "He probably had help to make his getaway."

Lucy sat up straighter when Niall appeared. The three brothers gathered in the hallway, close enough for her to eavesdrop on their conversation. "Then I'm guessing he's not a crazy. Most shooters like that work solo. They're expecting notoriety after the fact and don't care if they get caught or not. I've got a couple of guys at the lab combing social media to see if there's any kind of suicide note or manifesto posted. This guy had a purpose for being there."

"To take down Grandpa?" Keir asked.

Duff swore under his breath. "To take down someone. Either he's a lousy shot and Grandpa is collateral damage—"

"Or he hit exactly who he was aiming for," Niall concluded.

Thomas Watson entered the hallway after his sons. "And the man with the best shot at telling us why he was targeted can't talk."

The raised male voices were instantly shushed by a middle-aged woman sporting green scrubs and a honey-brown ponytail. She shut the door behind her and moved past them, speaking as if she expected the four men to follow her. "I thought the doctor made it very clear, Mr. Watson. No more than two visitors in the room at the same time. And only for a few minutes. And I find you all in there grilling him for information? You'll tire your father out."

Thomas lengthened his rolling stride to catch

up to the nurse's quick steps. "But he wants to see us. We have decisions to make about his care, and I want his input."

"Input?" The nurse stopped in the waiting area, unfazed by the circle of Watson men towering around her. "You asked him one question about hiring me, then went right back to your investigation. Seamus can't speak, and having him squeeze your hand so often to indicate yes and no is taxing on his fine-motor muscles and the neural transmitters he needs to slowly learn how to master all over again. You saw how agitated he was."

"We were reassuring him that we're staying on top of KCPD's investigation into his getting shot," Thomas explained. "He's a retired cop. He needs to hear that."

The nurse seemed unimpressed by his argument. "He needs to rest."

Millie stood with the baby. "Is Seamus all right?"

Thomas propped his hands at his waist, echoing the stance Lucy had seen Niall use so many times. "I think *frustrated* is the word for it, Millie. Clearly, his ideas and stubbornness are intact, but he's struggling to communicate what he means."

The nurse, whose name badge read Jane

Boyle, RN, tilted her face up to admonish Thomas. "Small steps, Mr. Watson. Your father needs to take small steps if he's going to recover fully. And if you intend to hire me, then we'll follow the doctor's orders and do exactly as I say with my patient. And that means no interrogations."

Niall's older brother, Duff, crossed his massive arms beside their father. "We haven't signed on the dotted line yet, lady."

Millie's voice sounded much older than it had just a few moments earlier. "You're hiring someone to take care of Seamus when he comes home?"

Thomas nodded. "Dr. Koelus said Dad needs round-the-clock care for a couple of weeks and physical therapy for some time beyond that. He recommended Ms. Boyle here. She's a private nurse with PT experience. But we're trying to decide if she and Seamus are compatible. Hell, we're trying to decide if she and I are compatible. If she's staying at the house…"

Millie's blue gaze darted over to Lucy, and she turned her head to whisper, "I think Tommy needs to be changed. Do you mind if I take him to the ladies' room?"

"Of course not. Do you want me to take him?"

"Don't be silly, dear. I can manage."

"Thank…you?" Although her nose hadn't detected any telltale odor, Lucy deferred to the older woman's experience. But when she handed her the diaper bag, Lucy read something else in Millie's eyes before she scurried away down the corridor. Of all the family meetings she'd imagined being a part of, they'd never included taking any member for granted. Perhaps worry and fatigue had clouded Niall's keen powers of observation. Or maybe it was a guy thing that all four men were oblivious to what was so painfully clear to Lucy.

Before Lucy could mention Millie's distress, Jane Boyle dismissed herself from the conversation. "I select my assignments very carefully, Mr. Watson. If I don't feel good about the patient's home environment, then I don't take the job."

"Home environment?" Thomas pointed a finger at the nurse. "Are you questioning my—"

"I'll be in Dr. Koelus's office for another ten minutes if you want to continue the interview. Then I'll be looking for my next potential assignment."

The younger brother, Keir, was a shorter, twenty-twenty version of Niall. He eased a low whistle between his teeth as the nurse brushed past him to turn the corner into the crossing hallway leading to the doctor's office. "You get a load of that lady? She's full of herself, isn't she?"

Duff needed a shave and something to take the edge off the wary tension surrounding him. "The fact that she didn't succumb to your questionable charm is the only thing she's got going for her."

"Hey, I get along great with older women. Isn't that right, Millie? Millie?" Keir turned to discover Lucy's new friend had disappeared. "Where did she go?"

"Is Tommy all right?" Niall asked, noting the baby's absence.

Lucy tilted her chin to see concerned looks on the faces of all four men. But it was Niall's probing gaze she answered. "The baby is fine. None of you have any clue to what just happened, do you? Millie cares about Seamus— she thinks of your family as her own."

Keir's blue eyes narrowed. "She *is* part of the family."

Lucy shrugged. "She might even have extra feelings for your grandfather."

"Extra?" Niall adjusted his glasses on the bridge of his nose, demanding clarification.

"I think she's sweet on him. Or whatever it

is that a woman in her seventies feels for an eighty-year-old man."

Duff scrubbed his fingers over the stubble of his beard. "She's got the hots for Grandpa?"

Thomas silenced him with a look and urged Lucy to continue.

"She certainly cares about him." Lucy gestured down the main hall to the room where Seamus Watson lay just a few doors away. "She hasn't even been allowed in to see him yet because, strictly speaking, she's not a relative."

"Of course she's family." Thomas shook his head as if her statement didn't make sense. "The two of them have lived in the same house for twenty years. I've been so preoccupied with Dad, convincing Olivia and Gabe to take some sort of honeymoon, and trying to make sense of the whole damn shooting—"

"You're not in this alone, Dad. We all dropped the ball." Niall reached over to squeeze his father's shoulder. But he was looking to Lucy for an answer. "How do we make it right?"

Lucy wasn't sure it was her place to interfere, but she was starting to get used to explaining people and emotions to her intellectual neighbor. "She's always taken care of all of you, right? I think she's hurt because you're hiring someone else to do her job."

Thomas muttered a rueful apology under his breath. "Ms. Boyle is a registered nurse. She'll be Dad's caretaker and physical therapist. I don't expect her to do anything else. And I'm certainly not kicking Millie out of the house."

"Don't tell me. Tell her. Let her know she's welcome, that she's important to each of you, that you still need her…even if it is just to cook and clean, or to spell the nurse when she needs a break. And she probably wants to be close to Seamus. She's feeling like there's nothing she can do to help right now."

Duff swore under his breath. "I can relate to that."

Thomas agreed. "We all can."

Lucy startled when Keir leaned over to kiss her cheek before thumping Niall's arm and leaving the carpeted waiting area. "Thank you. You know, I like that Niall's finally got a real live girlfriend."

"Oh, I'm not—"

"Excuse me?" Niall frowned at his brother's teasing assertion.

Keir ignored both protests and headed down the hallway. "I was beginning to think Dr. Frankenstein was going to have to build one in that lab of his."

"Where are you going?" Thomas asked.

"To find Millie. I'll take her to lunch and make amends, while you and Duff and that battle-ax Boyle make arrangements to take Grandpa home and get him set up." He turned, backing down the hallway without missing a step. "You *are* hiring her, right? I mean, who else is going to put up with his guff? She stood up to all of us, didn't she? Not an easy task, is it, Luce? You said what we needed to hear."

"I was just pointing out—" Keir winked at Lucy and then turned, including her in that sideways compliment before planting himself outside the ladies' restroom.

You need to learn to keep your mouth shut, Lucy Claire McKane. No man on this planet likes a woman who doesn't know when to zip it. Now you go right back to the Campbells' house and apologize to Roger.

"But Mama, he slapped me."

"Well, he wouldn't if you ever learned to stop talkin' when it's not your business. How he treats his own dog isn't your affair. And put on them tight jeans I got you before you go back to see him. Those curves will help him see how sorry he is for mistreatin' ya. He's a Campbell—the best ticket out of this two-bit town we're ever gonna get."

Lucy squeezed her eyes shut against the bile

rising in her gullet at the remembered incident. She'd never learned to keep her opinions to herself. And while, idealistically, she never regretted standing up for someone in need, she had learned to regret speaking those opinions without thinking through the consequences first.

Dropping her head, Lucy crossed back to the chair where she'd sat to go through her purse, ostensibly looking for something to busy her hands with until she could bury the painful flashback in her memories and concentrate on the present again—and how best to apologize to the Watsons for butting into their family business when they already had plenty on their plate to worry about.

With some sort of tacit agreement reached, Duff and Thomas followed Nurse Boyle around the corner to Dr. Koelus's office while Keir called someone on his cell phone and paced back and forth at the far end of the hall. Lucy pulled a tube of lip balm from her cosmetic bag and ran it around her mouth before she realized Niall was still standing behind her shoulder, staring down at her. She recognized that look, as though she was a specimen under a microscope he wanted to understand.

She dropped the lip balm back into her purse and turned, chin tipped up to meet his studious gaze. "What?" she asked, hearing a defensive edge to her tone she instantly wished she could take back. That only made him curious to ask more questions.

"You're avoiding me. Did Keir embarrass you with the girlfriend comment? He's a relentless teaser."

Those blue eyes were perfectly serious. Bless his stoic heart. The man could earn a medical degree and help solve crimes for the police department, but he still had no clue about the crush she'd had on him since their first meeting in the laundry room. Keir might have tuned in to her interest in his older brother, but she wasn't about to explain that attraction to Niall and risk the alliance they'd made for Tommy's and Diana's sakes. She also wasn't about to embarrass herself with any more details about her past than she'd shared with him earlier, either. "Don't worry. I know you and I are just friends. I hope I didn't overstep the boundaries of our agreement by butting in to your personal family business. Perhaps I didn't choose the best time to mention my suspicions about Millie."

He nodded, although what Niall was agreeing to, she couldn't be sure. "Keir was right about one thing. You have a real talent for reading people. You understand the subtleties of emotion in a way I never will."

"That's not true. I know you rely on that brain of yours, but you have good instincts, too." Lucy tucked a stray curl behind her ear and smiled up at him. "You knew where to find me last night when I needed you. And look at the bond between you and Tommy. You know when he needs you, too. I think he's already forming an emotional attachment to you. He senses you care about him."

Niall's gaze followed the movement of her hand. And then he surprised her by capturing one of the strands of hair that had curled beneath the neckline of her sweatshirt between two fingers and freeing it. She tried to dismiss the way he held on to the curl, arranging it just so behind her shoulder. It was probably just a scientist's impulse to have everything in a neat and tidy order, but her pulse was having other ideas. "I'm a calm presence, that's all. I'm guessing he's had a lot of upheaval in his young life."

Upheaval, yes. She could relate. With Lucy's pulse leaping at his curiously intimate touch, her words held double meaning. "Some people find security in that sort of quiet confidence."

"I hope he knows one day what a champion

you are for him." As he pulled away, Niall paused, brushing away the imaginary mark his brother's lips had left on her cheek.

If the tangle of his fingers in her hair hadn't been unsettling enough, the warm stroke of his thumb across her cool skin made her remember that pragmatic touch in front of the clothes dryer last night, and she shivered. Her words came out in an embarrassingly breathy stumble. "You are, too. A champion, I mean."

Niall's fingers splayed along the line of her jaw, his thumb lingering against the apple of her cheek. When his eyes narrowed behind his glasses and the distance between their heights disappeared, Lucy caught her breath in a gasp that was pure anticipation.

Lucy's awareness of the world around her— the bustle of hospital workers, the constant beeps and whirrs of medical equipment, and the medicinal smells wafting through the chilly air—shrank to the subtle pressure of Niall's warm mouth curving over hers. Her palm found a button at the middle of his shirt and settled there, balancing her as she tipped her head back to move her lips beneath his. They shared a quiet, deep kiss that heated Lucy's blood all the way down to her toes.

She wasn't sure when her heels left the floor

or when her fingers curled into the crisp cotton of his shirt, or even when her tongue boldly reached out to touch his. But Lucy was blatantly aware of her world shifting on its axis, of a two-year-old fantasy coming to life—of something stirring inside her that felt as dangerous as it was desirable. Niall Watson was kissing her. It was sweet and patient and thorough and perfect, made all the more sexy by how clueless he was of his masculine appeal. His mouth was an irresistible combination of tender purpose and firm demand. And that crazy heat he exuded that drew her like a moth to a flame—

An abrupt chill filled the air around her when Niall pulled his mouth from hers. His chest expanded against her hand as he drew in a deep breath and slowly exhaled. But his blue eyes remained locked on hers. "Was that all right? Your pupils dilated. Did I misread the signal you were sending? Or did I just interpret it the way I wanted to?"

"The signal? No. You read me just fine." Lucy pulled away from the tempting warmth radiating through the Oxford cloth she'd crinkled beneath her hand. She wished she wasn't blocked by the chair behind her or she'd put some serious distance between them while she gathered her wits. *Did I misread the signal?*

"Was that an experiment to test your people-reading skills?"

"An experiment?" He shook his head. "I wanted to thank you. Millie means a lot to me—to all of us."

"Oh. Of course. Glad I could help." Lucy managed a smile, salvaging some pride at the knowledge that her first, and most likely only, kiss with Niall Watson hadn't been in the name of science. Still, that tender exploration wasn't any admission of a mutual attraction. He'd intended to express his gratitude while she'd taken another step toward falling in love with the man. He probably thought her traitorous pupils and the goose bumps that prickled beneath the warm fingers still resting against her neck were some sort of involuntary response to the cold, filtered air inside the hospital. "I kind of specialize in creating healthy family relationships. It's the least I could do after all you're doing to help Tommy and Diana."

"Lucy—"

He opened his handsome mouth to say something more, but Thomas Watson appeared around the corner and called for his son to join them. "Niall. I'd like your two cents on this, too. Sorry. Am I interrupting?"

Lucy sidled away the moment Niall turned

to his father's bemused smile. "What do you need, Dad?"

"I thought you'd have a better idea of where we can fit all of Dad's medical equipment. There's more room in the guest suite, but if we have to accommodate Ms. Boyle for a few weeks, then she'll want a private bathroom—"

"You'd better go." Lucy gave Niall a nudge toward his father. "It's important."

He glanced over the jut of his shoulder at her. "So is this. I think there's been some kind of misunderstanding between us."

"Not at all. You said thank you, and I said you're welcome." They were friends, allies—and she was grateful for that. But a few minutes apart would allow her to clear her head of any of the misguided fantasies that were still firing through her imagination. "Looks like we might be at the hospital a little longer. Could I borrow your keys and get my knitting bag out of your car? It'll help me pass the time. Tommy will be fine with Millie until I get back."

After a momentary pause, he reached into the pocket of his jeans and handed them over. "Straight there and back, all right? If you overhear any arguments, call me before you go investigate on your own."

"I won't be gone more than ten minutes. Then I'll come back and spell Millie with the baby."

"Ten minutes," he clarified.

"Okay." She uttered the promise in as conversational a tone as she could muster, not wanting him to suspect just how eager she was to put some thought-clearing distance between them.

He didn't release the keys once she'd wrapped her fingers around them, holding on without actually touching her. "I haven't forgotten about Tommy and Diana. We'll go to the lab right after this."

"I know." She could never question his commitment to finding answers.

Lucy pocketed his keys and hurried to the elevator, knowing Niall continued to study her retreat, probably trying to make sense of her passionate response to a simple thank-you kiss. But she refused to look back and let him see the confusion and embarrassment that was no doubt evident on her face. Last night he'd touched her, more than once. They'd traded some full-body contact that had ignited more than a distant fantasy. And now he'd kissed her. With any other man—like that drunk in the disreputable neighborhood the police had dubbed no-man's-land—she'd think he was into her. But Niall Watson didn't quite understand the intricacies of attraction—and these increasingly intimate interactions that were wreaking havoc on her heart and hormones were nothing more than gratitude and practical necessities to Niall.

When the elevator opened, Lucy dashed inside and pushed the button for the lobby. When she did dare to look back across the hallway, she saw that she was still the object of Niall's piercing scrutiny. It wasn't until she held up ten fingers right before the doors shut that he finally turned away to Dr. Koelus's office. And it wasn't until she broke contact with those blue eyes that she was finally able to release a deep sigh of relief.

The elevator descended, and with each floor, a little more common sense returned. She was foolish for letting her feelings for Niall simmer into anything more than a stupid crush. Maybe these weren't real feelings, anyway. It made sense for a woman with her background to idolize a man who was the complete opposite of a volatile glory seeker like Roger Campbell, to be drawn to a man to whom family was so obviously important. But that didn't mean she was falling in love with the quiet mystery man across the hall. She had far more important things to worry about than her love life, anyway. Like finding Diana. Making sure Tommy felt safe and nurtured. Even just finishing the blue cap she was knitting for him.

When Lucy stepped outside the hospital's sliding glass doors, she was hit by a sharp blast of damp wind that cut through her sweatshirt and camisole, reminding her that she'd been in such a hurry to escape before Niall started grilling her with questions she didn't want to answer, that she'd left without her sweater coat. Spring was trying to come to Kansas City, but it wasn't here yet. Although the temperature was well above freezing, the drab day did little to perk up her spirits. She crossed her arms in front of her and surveyed the dingy landscape of sooty snow melting against the curb and the muddy mess of brown grass surrounding a few denuded trees. Even the evergreen shrubs had a grayish cast that reflected the low, overcast sky.

Maybe the promised rain would wash away the last dregs of winter and she wouldn't worry quite so much about Diana being out in this. Was money the reason she'd left Tommy with her? There'd been nothing with the infant but the clothes on his back. She and Niall and Thomas Watson had bought or borrowed everything Tommy could need. But did Diana have a warm coat to wear? A safe place to stay out of the weather? Food to eat? Did she know how much Lucy ached to see her foster daughter's beautiful smile and hug her in her arms again?

Warmth of a different kind trickled down Lucy's cheek and she quickly wiped the tear away. Crying wouldn't do Diana or Tommy any good. And she certainly didn't need to embarrass herself any further by standing here in front of a big city hospital crying her eyes out, especially after that humiliating lapse in judgment with Niall upstairs.

Shaking off both the cold and the negativity of her fatigue-fueled thoughts, Lucy crossed the driveway and followed the sidewalk around to Saint Luke's visitors' parking lot. She found Niall's SUV easily enough and slung the long strap of her knitting bag over her shoulder and across her chest before locking it again.

Glimpsing a distorted movement reflecting off the side window, she shut the back door and swung around. She slowly released the breath that had locked up in her chest and nodded to the older couple walking past the rear bumper. Of course. It was probably them that she'd seen, reflecting at a weird angle as they approached and then passed Niall's SUV. After that close call outside their condominium building last night, she was probably being extra paranoid about silver cars and parking lots. Still, it was hard to shake the sense that there was something unseen just beyond the corner of her eye, something that she was missing.

A shiver skittered down her spine that had nothing to do with the penetrating breeze. Had she imagined the car following her? Or simply confused another resident's new vehicle with something similar she'd seen down in no-man's-land? Holding the strap of her knitting bag in both fists, she walked to the rear of the SUV and looked up and down the lane of parked cars. Was someone watching her? She seemed to have a sixth sense for when Niall was studying her, and she lifted her gaze to the hospital's fifth floor. Was he spying on her from the waiting-area windows, making sure she didn't disappear before all the mysteries swirling through that brilliant head of his could be solved? Lucy frowned. All the glass on the front of the building reflected the sea of clouds, making it impossible to tell if anyone inside was overly curious about her. Best to get moving and go back inside.

Although she felt fairly certain that neither Roger nor the drunk from the aptly named no-man's-land Thomas Watson had described would have any clue how to track her to this part of the city, she still found herself looking at all the cars she passed as she hurried across the parking lot. She was specifically looking for a silver sports car, but it was daunting to see exactly how many gray and silver vehicles there were in the parking lot, and impossible to know whether any of the people walking in and out of Saint Luke's main doors belonged to one of those cars or if anyone, seen or unseen, was watching her.

The uneasy suspicion remained when she re-entered the hospital's lobby and moved through the main visitors' area to the bank of elevators. Maybe it was just the chill of the dreary February air staying with her. Maybe that's why she'd felt someone's eyes on her—they'd thought she was a fool for venturing outside without mittens or a cap or even so much as an umbrella to ward off the coming rain.

The elevator doors opened, and Lucy watched with an envious tug on her heart as a nurse pushed out a wheelchair with a new mom holding her baby while the dad and a big brother and sister followed them with balloons and flowers and a basket of gifts. And though she managed a smile and "Congratulations" to the expanding family, Lucy's arms tightened around her middle. That was never going to happen for her.

Roger Campbell and her mother had seen to that. Despite her good fight to remain optimistic, a gloom as chilly and blah as the weather outside settled around her shoulders.

Once the elevator was clear, Lucy stepped inside. She had five floors to push the past out of her head and fix a legitimate smile on her face for Niall and Tommy and Millie and the Watsons and the rest of the world she intended to take on until she located Diana and reunited her with Tommy. She retreated to the back rail as two men converged on the waiting elevator, giving them space to come in. But the younger man darted past the gentleman carrying a bouquet of flowers, pushing a button as he slipped inside.

"Hey, I think that guy wanted—" The young man pushed the close button with rapid-fire repetition, nearly catching the other man's outstretched hand between the sliding doors before he wisely pulled back to wait for the next car. "Okay."

Guess you're in a hurry.

Lucy arched an eyebrow at his rudeness and kept her distance from the preoccupied man. With his back to her and the collar of his leather jacket turned up, masking all but the top of his coal-black hair, she could only speculate whether fear for a loved one's health or excitement over a new birth or simply being self-centered were what drove him to get to where he needed to go so quickly. She couldn't even see around him to find out what floor number he'd pushed. But he certainly smelled good—if one liked the scents of Italian cooking that filled the elevator. He must be a chef or come from a family who—

"You were downtown yesterday, asking about Diana Kozlow?"

Lucy's wandering thoughts smashed into the steel door of reality. Her gaze shot to his up-turned collar and her heart raced with a wary excitement. "You know Diana? Can you help me?" She took a step forward but quickly retreated to the far corner of the car when he shifted his back to her, not only to keep his face hidden, but to expose the sheath of a long knife, strapped to the waist of his dark jeans. "Where can I find her?"

"You need to stop asking questions." His accent, a mix of guttural consonants and rolling *r*'s, reminded her of the argument outside her laundry room and the answering machine message at her office.

"Were you at my building last night? Was Diana with you?" Was he the man Diana had sounded so afraid of on the answering machine? Had he hurt her? Had he threatened her with that knife? Hell, he wasn't that much taller than Lucy, but he was muscular enough to do damage with his bare hands.

His only answer was a terse "Shut up. You're only making it worse."

"Making what worse?" She desperately wanted him to answer. "Who are you? Is Diana okay? Where is she?" One answer. Any answer. She was beginning to understand Niall's obsession with resolving loose ends. "Please. She's like a daughter to me. I just need to see her and know she's okay. Can you help me? I need to talk to her."

His shoulders hunched inside his jacket, and he exhaled an audible groan of what—impatience? Frustration? "What about the baby?"

He knew about the baby? "Tommy is hers, isn't he?"

"Tommy?" The man angled his face partway toward hers, although she still couldn't make out much more than olive skin with beads of sweat making the black strands of hair stick to his forehead.

"Tell me the baby's real name. What does Diana call him?"

"Is he safe? He is well?" Was that a wistful note in his cryptic words?

He cared about Tommy. He *knew* Tommy. "Yes. Didn't you see him last night? I think Diana did. He needs his mother. Can you take me to her?"

"Tommy is a good name. Whatever you do, don't let that baby out of your sight. And don't let him anywhere near Diana again."

Again? Diana *was* the woman who'd left the lipstick kiss on Tommy's forehead. "How can I? I don't know where she is. What's going on? Did you break into my apartment? Wait. What kind of car do you drive?" The elevator slowed its ascent and stopped with a soft bounce. She glanced up. Fourth floor. He was getting off without telling her anything except veiled threats that made her even more afraid for Diana. "Please. Is she okay?" He slipped between the sliding doors before they were fully open. Forgetting the knife and the muscles, she lunged forward and grabbed his arm to stop him. "I just want to talk—"

He winced and muttered a foreign curse before he jerked free of her grip and shoved her back into the elevator. Lucy barely caught a glimpse of dark eyes and sharp cheekbones before he reached back in to push the door-close button.

"Hey. Hey!" She clipped her elbow on the steel railing, sending a tingle of momentary numbness down to her fingertips, before landing on her bottom. But she ignored the bruising pain and scrambled to the control panel to reverse the command. She caught the door as it stopped, then opened again, narrowing her gaze on the bloody palm print sliding out of sight between the elevator and outside wall.

Confused shock stopped her for a moment. That was *her* palm print. The blood was on *her* hand.

But she wasn't bleeding.

The mysterious man was injured.

And he was getting away.

"Hey, stop!" The staff and visitors walking the hall paused and turned as she rushed out. "Come back!"

"Miss?" A black man wearing a white lab coat over his tie and dress slacks put a hand on her arm. "Are you all right?"

She twisted away, taking a step one direction, then the opposite, looking for a leather coat. "Did you see a man get off the elevator? A dark-haired man?"

The woman beside him also wore a lab coat and carried a tablet computer. "Are you hurt?"

"I'm fine. There was a man in the elevator. He must have been running."

"This is Dr. McBride," the woman introduced her companion. "Do you need him to look at that hand?"

"No." Lucy flashed a smile and dismissed their concern. "This is his blood. I have to find him."

"Him?"

"Did you see—" An elevator beeped beside the one she'd exited. "Do you know if that's going up or down?"

The woman shrugged an apology as Dr. McBride asked, "What's the man's name?"

"I have no idea. I've never met him before."

The doctor crossed to the nurses' station and ordered them to notify security about the injured man.

"Do you need to wash up?" his assistant offered.

"No. I need to find…" Lucy's gaze zeroed in on the door marked Stairway gently closing and took off at a run. "Excuse me."

She pushed open the door and stopped on the concrete landing, glancing up and down, adjusting her hearing to the sudden quiet compared to the noises and voices out on the hospital floor. There. Footsteps running down the stairs.

"Wait!" she shouted, hurrying down the steel and concrete stairs. "I need your help."

Lucy wasn't an athlete by any stretch of the imagination, but she'd walked miles on the treadmill in the gym back in her building, so she pushed herself to move faster and catch the man before he exited the hospital. She slung her bag behind her back and balanced her hand against the railing, leaving her bloody mark as she spun around one landing and the next. She was nearly breathless, as much from desperation as from her sprint down four flights, when she burst through the stairwell exit onto the sidewalk outside.

"Where…" So many cars. Too many people. Too many bushes and trees.

Lucy almost headed over to the main entrance to see if the man who'd given her the cryptic warning had taken a turn somewhere and come out into the main lobby. But then she saw the small red blob seeping into the sidewalk a few feet away. She jogged out to the edge of the driveway, spotted another blood droplet on the opposite curb and hurried across into the main parking lot. There. A spot on the fender of someone's car. Another one on the white arrow marking the turn lane to the exit. She wasn't aware of the gray sky anymore, was barely aware of the damp chill in the air as she hurried behind the bloody trail. She was nearly to the road at the far end of the parking lot when the path she was following ended.

"No." Her nostrils flared as she took a deep breath to slow her panic. "You're my best lead." She scanned the grassy brown berm for one more clue to finding the man, praying she hadn't reached a dead end. "Help me. Help…"

Lucy looked up and saw an orangey-red pickup truck, its noisy engine idling and sending out plumes of stinky exhaust as it waited to turn onto the hilly road that ran in front of Saint Luke's. She saw the driver, staring at her through the window.

Dark hair. Brown eyes. Sad brown eyes.

Lucy's heart leaped in her chest. "Diana!"

The how and the why didn't matter. Overwhelming relief gave her a second wind. Lucy charged up the hill.

"Diana!" The young woman splayed her fingers against the glass, turning away and shaking her head. Was that a wave goodbye? "No. Wait!"

She saw the blur of movement between two parked cars a second too late.

"I said to leave us alone!"

She caught a glimpse of shiny gray steel before something hard struck her in the temple, spinning the world around her. Lucy crumpled to her hands and knees as the man in the leather jacket charged past her.

Her jeans and sweatshirt were soaking up the moisture from the grass by the time she heard the squeal of tires against the pavement and her world faded from gray to black.

Chapter Six

Niall would allow Lucy ten minutes to come back from her errand.

At eleven minutes, he excused himself from the meeting with his father and Jane Boyle, which had somehow devolved into a discussion about overstepping personal boundaries and who'd be in charge of what once she moved in to care for Seamus. Leaving the two of them to butt heads, Niall went back to the waiting area, looking for dark curls and a knitting bag but finding neither. Adjusting his glasses on the bridge of his nose, he scanned up and down the hallway. No Lucy. Something was wrong.

Although he still hadn't figured out why she'd pulled away from that kiss—and hadn't even had time to fully process the impulse that had prompted him to put his fingers in her hair and taste every inch of her rosy lips in the first place when a verbal thank-you would have sufficed perfectly well—there were two things he knew for certain about Lucy McKane: she was a woman of her many words, and she didn't want to be away from Tommy any longer than was necessary. If she'd promised to be right back, she should be here by now. She would be with the baby.

While assessing his options and formulating a plan, Niall rubbed his palm on the thigh of his jeans, trying to erase the memory of Lucy's silky curls twisting around his fingers as if they'd grabbed hold of him with the same enthusiasm her grip against his chest had. He needed to concentrate on the clues around him and figure out his best plan of action. Realizing her purse and cell phone were still sitting there in the chair where she'd left them, and that calling her wasn't an option, he quickly moved on to plan B.

Spying Keir and Millie conversing outside the ladies' room, Niall strode down the hallway to join them. "Is Lucy in there?"

Millie shifted back and forth on her feet, rocking the cooing infant on her shoulder. "No. Tommy and I were the only ones in there. I haven't seen Lucy since we left."

"Keir, have you seen her?" Niall wondered at

the little gut punch of satisfaction when Tommy shifted his alert brown eyes to him at the sound of his voice.

"No, bro." Keir gave him a playful punch on the arm. "Aw, come on. I liked her. You haven't scared her off already, have you?" His teasing grin quickly faded when he didn't get a rise out of Niall. "Hey, just kidding. Is something wrong?"

Niall couldn't wait here and play negotiator while his father and Ms. Boyle tried to reach a compromise. And he sure as hell didn't have time to be responsible for keeping Duff's mouth shut in there to prevent a serious rift between the family and the woman they needed to see to their grandfather's recovery. Instead, he took Millie's arm and walked her toward Seamus's room. "Are you okay watching Tommy a little longer?"

"Of course. What's happened, Niall?"

"Lucy went out to the car. She should have been back by now."

"She said she thought someone had been following her the past couple of days. Do you think he found her?"

"What?" Niall stopped and looked down into Millie's crinkled blue eyes. "Who's following her?"

"She didn't know. Someone in a silver car."

"Ah, hell. There was a car like that at our building last night. Silver Camaro. Nearly ran her over."

Millie wrapped her hand around the back of Tommy's head, as if she didn't want him to hear this surprising tidbit of news. "She said she spotted it downtown when she was looking for her foster daughter and then again about a block from your building. She didn't mention anything about last night."

"Probably because she didn't want to upset you," Keir suggested. "But if this guy has located where she lives and saw you two leaving this morning—"

"He could have tracked us to her office and then the hospital." Niall raked his fingers through his hair, berating himself for making such a rookie mistake. "I wasn't even looking for something like that."

"When you work a crime, you're used to the people being dead, not chasing after you," Keir pointed out. "It's been a long time since your academy training."

"That's no excuse."

"Maybe it's her foster daughter, trying to make contact again," Millie suggested.

Niall doubted it. "Or the creep trying to hurt Diana and Tommy."

Keir was the detective here. He pulled out his phone. "I can do a search for silver Camaros in Kansas City. If you're thinking about tracking one down without a license plate or even make and model, though, it'll be a long shot. Maybe we can narrow down the search grid to certain neighborhoods."

Niall nodded and resumed walking. He wondered why Lucy hadn't mentioned seeing the Camaro more than once when she'd seemed so open about everything else, including some disturbing hints regarding her past. If someone had been following her, that could explain her instinct to punch first and ask questions later, or run outside to confront whoever was tailing her.

When they reached room number 5017, he pushed open the door and ushered them inside. He dropped the diaper bag on a chair and crossed to the bed where Seamus Watson lay. The old man's bright blue eyes tracking Niall's movements were the only color in his wan face. "Grandpa, I brought someone to keep you company." He leaned over and kissed Seamus's forehead beside the layers of gauze that covered the bullet hole and surgical incision there. "I have to go to work. Millie's going to introduce you to little Tommy. He belongs to a friend. He's..." He palmed the small, warm head resting on Millie's shoulder. Tommy's eyes looked up at him, too. "...a baby."

Seamus's eyes opened as wide as the stroke would let him, and his lips fluttered with a remembered task. Clearly, there was a question there.

But Niall didn't have time to answer. He headed for the door before he lost his focus again. With Lucy's penchant for being led by her instincts and emotions and not thinking things through, she could be in real trouble. "Millie will explain."

Keir stopped him at the door. "You want backup?"

"No." They still had no leads on their grandfather's shooting—whether it was an accidental hit, or if somebody would be coming back to finish the job. And he couldn't focus on two mysteries that hit so close to home at the same time. "I need to know these people are safe."

Keir pulled back the front of his jacket, tapping his belt beside the badge and sidearm holstered there. "They will be. I'll find out what I can about the car."

With a nod, Niall strode from the room.

When he got on the elevator, he was more certain than ever that something was terribly wrong. A crimson palm print, half the size of his own, stared at him from the closed steel door. He inhaled a deep breath to counteract the rush of unaccustomed anger that heated his blood. It wasn't necessarily Lucy's. The blood didn't mean she was hurt. His gaze dropped to the number-four button and the smudge of a bloody fingerprint marking it. It was too big to come from the hand that marked the door.

There'd been two people on this elevator. A man and a woman. And at least one of them was seriously injured.

Ah, hell. Niall pushed the button, stopping the elevator at the next floor. When the doors opened, he stepped out. "Lucy?"

A quick visual sweep of the people moving on the fourth floor revealed no curly-haired brunette. But two security guards were converging on the nurses' station. Niall held up his badge as he approached the doctor standing there. "Have you seen a dark-haired woman? Thirtyish? Wearing a Royals sweatshirt?"

The other man turned from the guards he was giving a report to. "She was here a few minutes ago. She said there was an injured man on the elevator. Last I saw she was heading—"

Niall didn't need to hear the rest. A second scan picked up the elongated blood drops on the tiles leading to the stairwell exit. Directional spatter. Whoever had been injured on the elevator was running—away from someone or after someone, he couldn't tell. Logic indicated that one of them had to be Lucy.

The blood left a clear trail down the stairs. Too much of a trail. Niall took the stairs at a jog, skipping two steps at a time, burning inside at the idea any drop of it could be Lucy's.

He found another bloody print on the door handle leading outside and pushed it open. "Lucy?"

A half dozen people on the front sidewalk turned at his shout. Not her. None of them were her.

A sprinkling of rain spotted his glasses. He looked through the drops to zero in on the next bloodstain on the opposite curb. Even with the growing intensity of the rain, thinning the spot into rivulets that washed away in the gutter, he could tell that the blood marks were getting bigger, more circular. Whoever was injured was slowing down, succumbing to his or her wound. The instinct to run to his truck and grab his kit to preserve some of the blood so he could ID its owner blipped into his brain and out just as quickly when he saw four or five people converging at the far edge of the parking lot.

Good Samaritans running to help.

Help whom?

"Lucy? Lucy!" Niall stretched his long legs into a run, zigzagging between parked cars until he saw the woman on her hands and knees wearing muddy clothes and the people helping her to her feet. When she turned to thank one, he got a clear glimpse of the sticky red substance matting the hair beside that warm, velvety cheek. Niall had his badge in his hand by the time he reached the group and moved them aside. "KCPD crime lab. I'm a doctor."

"Niall." Lucy reached out her hands and tumbled into him as the others stepped back. He caught her in his arms and sat her down on the curb. Why was she smiling? Was she delirious? How bad was that head wound? "I saw her. I saw Diana. She was right here. She's alive."

"I'm tired of seeing you muddy and beat up. Where are you hurt? What happened?"

She was urging him to retreat as much as clinging to his arm for support. "We're getting wet. Where's your car? If we don't hurry we'll lose her again—"

"Stop talking." He quickly assessed her injuries, pushing her back onto her bottom and kneeling beside her when she tried to use him to stand again. The blood on her hand was washing away as the skies opened up and the rain began to fall in sheets around them. No cut or scrape there. But she winced as he pushed the damp curls away from her temple and saw the ugly gash in her hairline where the skin had split open. He pulled a white handkerchief from his back pocket and pressed it against the wound.

"Ow. Damn it, Niall, you need to listen to me."

"Can you see this?" He held up a finger in front of her face and moved it from side to side, watching her green eyes track the movement.

"Of course I can. There's nothing wrong with my eyesight. I *saw* Diana. She was right there." Since there was no obvious indication of a concussion, Niall shifted his attention, running his hand along her shoulders, elbows, hands, knees, ensuring there were no other injuries needing immediate attention. "Let me up. I'm soaked to the skin. We have to do something. Have you heard a word I've said?"

Niall was obliquely aware of a break in the rain hitting the top of his head as Duff ran up beside him. "Oh, hell. Is she all right?" A quick glance up to his big brother asked for an explanation and thanked him at the same time. Duff understood. "Keir called me. Said there might be a problem. What do you need?"

"Have you got a handkerchief on you?" Duff pulled a blue bandanna from his pocket. Niall wrapped it around the cuff of Lucy's sweatshirt and tied it off, trying to preserve some of the blood that had soaked in there. Since she had no injury to her hand or wrist, he suspected it would match the bloody fingerprint in the elevator and possibly give him a name for the culprit who had cracked her head open. "Look for a silver Camaro. Someone's been following her."

Lucy shook her head, dislodging the compress that stuck to the wound at her temple and moaning at the sudden movement. "No, Diana drove away in a red pickup truck. I mean, yes, there was a car yesterday. And last night. But just now...they turned north. Diana and the man from the elevator. They left together."

"What man?" Duff asked, pulling out his notepad and pen.

"He warned me not to try to find Diana. But I did. They were here together."

"Can you describe him?"

"He was bleeding." That made sense. Lucy's blood was redder, fresher, than the mess he'd found inside. Niall plucked up the soiled handkerchief from the shelf of her breasts. It was already getting too wet to do much good as a compress, so he used it to dab at the bruising and swelling so he could get a clearer look at the wound there. "He warned me not to try to find her. But she was here. She saw me…and then he…" She pushed Niall's hands away. "It's hard to think when you're doing that."

"I need to see how badly you're hurt."

"It's not my blood."

He held up the blood-soaked handkerchief. "The hell it isn't!"

"Easy, Niall." Duff rested his big hand on Niall's shoulder and knelt down beside him to talk to Lucy. "Can you give me a description of the truck?"

Lucy's wide eyes had locked on to Niall's at his irrational outburst. But she blinked away the raindrops glistening on her dark lashes and turned to Duff. "Faded red. Rusted around the wheel wells. Small. But I never saw a license plate. I didn't think to read it at the time, but it had words and a logo on the side of the door— like a business name."

Duff jotted down the information while Niall tried to ignore the irony of Lucy's calm recitation of facts when he'd been the one distracted by his emotional reactions. "And the guy?" Duff asked.

"Black hair. Black leather jacket and jeans. Mediterranean looking. He smelled like a restaurant, if that helps."

Duff pushed to his feet and turned to the people who'd gathered around to make sure Lucy was all right. "Did anybody else see the truck or the man who hit her?"

He took statements from a couple of bystanders who'd stayed to make sure she was all right. But Niall had collected his thoughts enough to understand they had little to add beyond confirming the details Lucy had shared. "Your perp has lost a lot of blood, too. He couldn't risk coming to this hospital, but he'll have to go somewhere for treatment soon or you'll be looking for a dead body."

"I'll put a call out to notify area hospitals and clinics. I'll check in when I know something." Duff pulled out his phone and punched in a number as Niall pulled Lucy to her feet. "You'll get her to the ER?" Niall nodded. "Sorry this happened, Luce. Stay strong. We'll find him. And don't let this guy scare ya too much."

Duff jogged away while Niall wrapped an arm around Lucy's waist and pulled her to his side, shielding her from the rain while keeping her close enough to hold the compress to her temple. "Let's get you inside."

Although the man in him was certainly aware of her sweetly rounded curves pressed against his body, the doctor in him was concerned about the chill he felt through the wet clothing where denim and cotton rubbed together. He tried to quicken her pace, but he had to shorten his stride when he felt her fingers dancing at the right side of his waist looking for a place to hold on to for balance. Finally, she slipped her cold thumb beneath the waistband of his jeans and latched on to a belt loop. "You know, sometimes I forget you're a cop as well as an ME. With your gun there, I'm not sure where to put my hand."

"You hang on anywhere you can. I've got you."

Three more steps, then a hesitation to blink the rain from her eyes, then another step. "Why would your brother think I'm scared of you? I'm not, you know. I mean, I get frustrated…" She tried to laugh, but the sound ended up more like a groan and she stopped, laying her hand over his on her forehead. "Okay, I guess I am hurt."

"Could we keep moving?" he suggested.

They made it past the next row of cars before

she stopped again. "Wait a minute. Where's Tommy? Is he okay? That man knew about him. He said not to let Tommy out of my sight. And I don't even know where he is."

"Tommy's fine. He's with Keir and Millie. He's meeting Grandpa. He'll be safe with them." She smiled, and he took a little more of her weight and pulled her into step beside him again.

"That's sweet. And Millie got to see Seamus. A visit like that will make all three of them feel better. Thank you for listening. And taking the time to come help me. Again. I know I said I'd be right back, but I couldn't pass up the chance to learn something about Diana. Oh, wow. You don't even have your jacket. You're getting so wet."

Chatty woman. Sometimes, he enjoyed the melodic sound of her voice filling up the silences he was far too accustomed to. But was there anyone she wasn't going to mention before she started taking care of herself? Or was the rambling an indication of some undetected head trauma?

Barely missing a step, he reached down behind her knees and swung her up into his arms, knitting bag and all. "Too much talking and not enough walking."

"Put me down."

He ignored the protest of her hands pressing against his chest and quickened his pace, carrying her straight to the hospital's main entrance. They could reach the ER through the lobby. "Put your arm around my neck and keep pressure on that wound."

Instead of obeying his instructions, she squiggled against him, trying to free herself from his grasp. "I can't afford to be an invalid, Niall. You do realize that I'm the only family Diana has. I mean, we can't exactly count Tommy when it comes to helping out. We're not like your family where your dad and your brothers and Millie and all your lab and cop friends jump in and help out. It's just me. I *have* to be there for her."

So what was he in all this? Who was ignoring the breast squeezed against his chest and the rain smearing his glasses to keep her from bleeding until she fell unconscious? Who'd rescued Tommy from hours alone without food or attention, or torn a hole in his UCM sweatpants saving her from that speeding car last night? Who'd agreed to team up with her for the baby's sake? How was she alone? "I swear to God, woman, if you don't stop talking, I'm going to kiss you again, just to keep you quiet."

"What? I…oh." Her struggles against him ceased. "Yes, Dr. Watson. Sorry to inconvenience you." Her arm crept around his neck, and she moved the wet compress back to her temple. "Shutting up now."

The receptionist at the front desk was on her feet to meet them. An orderly with a wheelchair joined him halfway down the long hallway that led into the emergency wing. Niall was aware that Lucy had stopped talking, doing exactly as he'd asked, except to give brief answers to the medical staff attending her. With her skin so pale and her eyes refusing to make contact with his, Niall made the decision not to prompt her into conversation, partly because he didn't want to upset her further and partly because he had no idea what he had done to make her shut down in the first place. Well, he had a good idea that he'd let his frustrations get the better of him and he'd said the wrong thing.

But was she mad at him? Hurt? Tired? Did she not see he was doing what needed to be done in order to keep her safe so that she *could* be there for both Diana and Tommy?

Niall gave a quick account of his assessment and what he'd done to treat Lucy's injury to the attending staff, then phoned his brothers to report on Lucy's condition and find out, as he'd expected, that there simply wasn't enough information yet to pinpoint the owner of either the silver car or the rusted red pickup. Was that why she had her nose out of joint—that he'd had someone to call on for help in a difficult situation? Didn't she understand that his family was helping her, too? And why, why, why did Lucy McKane get in his head like this and fill it up with so many unanswered questions?

He desperately needed to lose himself in the provable logic of his work and restore the equilibrium inside him. While Duff and Keir continued to make calls, Niall put on a dry shirt from his go bag and got his ME kit from the SUV to take pictures and secure blood samples before the hospital cleaning staff disinfected the elevator and stairwell. Whatever evidence might be outside had already been compromised by the rain, so he focused his attention on the evidence he *could* collect.

Lucy sat propped up on an examination table in one of the ER bays, wearing a hospital gown and shivering beneath the heated blanket draped over her lap when Niall returned nearly an hour later. He stood back for several seconds, watching her study her own toes wiggling fretfully beneath the edge of the blanket while an intern on the stool beside her tied off another stitch in her scalp. Did the woman have an inability to truly be still? Or was that her way of coping with the pain and discomfort she must be feeling?

The younger man acknowledged Niall as soon as he set his kit down on a chair just inside the curtain. "You were right about there not being a concussion, Dr. Watson. Looks like whatever he hit her with was small and the injury was localized."

The edema surrounding the wound gave a clear impression of the instrument used in the attack. Aware of Lucy's green eyes shifting from her purple-polished toenails to his every movement, Niall pulled his camera from his kit and snapped a few pictures before the intern put in the last two stitches. He enlarged the image on the camera screen. "Looks like a weapon about an inch wide, with a distinctive ridge pattern to it."

After tying off the last stitch, the intern placed his suture kit on a rolling stainless steel tray and ripped open a package of gauze with his sterile gloves. "Maybe the butt of a gun?"

Lucy tugged on Niall's wrist, pulling the camera down so that she could look at the image, too. "Or the handle of a knife?"

No comment on the puffy swelling beside

her right eye or the gray-and-violet bruise that marred her pale skin? She was an expert on wound markings now? Niall adjusted his glasses on the bridge of his nose. "It's not a cut. Blunt-force trauma split the skin open."

She opened her mouth to explain her comment, but the doctor was giving her directions to care for the wound. "When the anesthetic wears off, you're going to be pretty sore. It's okay to use an ice pack for the swelling, but don't let the stitches get wet. And no aspirin or ibuprofen for twenty-four hours or so." Young Dr. Shaughnessy, according to his name badge, peeled off his gloves and tossed them onto the tray as he rolled it over to the counter, where he typed something on to his laptop. "Since your tetanus shot is current, I think we can forgo the antibiotics. But if you do see any signs of an infection setting in, give us a call or contact your personal physician."

"I'll monitor her recovery," Niall assured the younger man.

With a nod, the intern picked up a plastic bag and handed it to Niall. "We bagged her clothes like you requested. I wouldn't leave them in there too long or they'll start to mildew. I took the liberty of labeling it and signing my name to preserve the chain of custody. I start my forensic rotation next month," he added with a slightly boyish enthusiasm.

"Thanks." Niall scanned the sealed bag and quickly scrawled his name beneath John Shaughnessy's. A pointed glare from Lucy seemed to indicate that something more needed to be said. She was still putting someone else before her own well-being. Niall frowned, but acquiesced to the silent demand. "Good luck with that."

"Thank you, sir. I might run into you at the ME's office then. Here's a clean set of scrubs you can change into." Dr. Shaughnessy handed that bag to Lucy. "Take your time, ma'am. Unfortunately, we're having a run of business this afternoon. I'd better go get my next assignment. Have a good one."

"Thanks, John." Before the curtains had even closed behind the intern, Lucy was squiggling off the edge of the table. "I've been here way too long. I keep thinking about how everything would be different if I'd just gotten Diana to talk to me."

When her toes hit the floor, she swayed and Niall reached across the table to steady her. But she put her hand up to keep him away.

"It's a bump on the head and a couple of stitches." Technically, Niall had counted seven.

But if she still wanted to keep some distance between them the way she had after that kiss upstairs and battle of wills outside, he'd respect the patient's wish. After he retreated a step, she dumped out the bag with the scrubs onto the exam table and pulled out a pair of white cotton socks. "I've just been off my feet too long. I need to get the circulation going again. Not to mention that it's freezing in here. I think my blood stopped flowing half an hour ago."

When she bent over to slide the first sock on, the gown split open at the back and gave him a clear view of her underwear clinging to the curves of her hips and bottom. He remembered those panties from the laundry she'd been folding late one night. They were a pretty lavender color, a few shades lighter than the polish on her toes, and Niall's groin tightened with an unexpected response that was as potent as it was ill timed. Niall politely turned away from the tempting sight. He needed something to focus on besides the way Lucy McKane was transforming his well-ordered world into a topsy-turvy mess.

"Tell me about the knife," he stated, maybe a little more harshly than he intended. "Tell me everything."

After a moment's hesitation, Lucy went back

to dressing and Niall went back to being a medical examiner with ties to KCPD's crime lab. He heard about the silver car that she'd seen in no-man's-land and again just a block from their condo building—and yes, she thought it could be the same car that had nearly run her down last night. She told him about the brute in the elevator and the long knife he'd carried that could explain the distinct pattern of her head wound. When Niall thought he had his physiological and emotional reactions well in check again, he pulled a narrow file from his kit and scraped the dried blood from beneath her fingernails and labeled it as evidence. In the back of his mind, he kept thinking how much easier it was to process a dead body in the lab than to deal with the scents of rain and blood and antiseptic on a living person. On a friend. On a woman who was the most alive person he'd ever dealt with.

On Lucy McKane.

Niall shook his head, warding off the uncharacteristic anger that simmered in his veins when he snapped a picture of the ugly bruise on her elbow and she told him how she'd followed the trail of blood the same way he had to track down the man who'd assaulted her and warned her to mind her own business. But when she raised her arms to slip into the pink scrub top, his temper boiled over. "Hold it."

Lucy froze at the sharpness in his voice and instinctively hugged the top to her waist. "What now?"

It wasn't the smooth curves of her lavender bra that had caught his attention, but the fist-size bruise turning all shades of purple framed between her breasts that had him circling around the exam table to stand directly in front of her. "Did he do that to you, too?"

A rosy blush dotted her cheeks as she tilted her face up to his. She turned away and lifted the shirt up over her head again before answering. "I suppose so. On the elevator when he shoved me back inside to get away."

Niall raised his camera. "I'd better get a shot of that, too."

She whirled around on him. "I am not a crime scene!"

"It's what I know how to do, Lucy. It's how I can help." Okay, so maybe going on seventy-two hours with hardly any sleep was giving him a short fuse he'd never had before, but the tear she swiped off her cheek and the soft gasp of pain wasn't helping him clear his head, either. "Apparently, I can't keep you from getting hurt, but I can analyze the size of his hand

and the weapon he carries. If I can get a clean sample of his blood off you and your clothes, maybe I can identify him. If I get DNA and he's in the system, I can send Duff and Keir to arrest him, and he won't be able to hurt you or threaten Tommy and Diana anymore."

"And if he's not?"

Niall slipped his fingers into his hair and scratched at the frustration jamming his thoughts. "I'm not up to that part of the plan yet."

"What plan is that?"

He threw out his hands and glared down at her. "The one where I keep you and Tommy safe and stuff like this doesn't happen."

Had that outburst really just come from him?

A gentle touch to his jaw snapped him out of his roiling thoughts. Lucy's lips were almost smiling when she reached up to stroke the spiky strands of hair off his forehead. He calmed at her tender caress. "I'll be okay, Niall. I've been hurt worse than this."

"Is that supposed to make me feel better?" There. He'd admitted it out loud. Maybe he'd just admitted it to himself. He was *feeling*. The visual of Lucy's injury and the touch of her hand made him feel emotions that were unexpected, and clearly more powerful than he was equipped to handle.

Yet with a smile he craved as much as her touch, she seemed to take every mood swing in stride. "You know, I was processed like this when I was seventeen. Back in Falls City."

"Processed? You were assaulted?" Parts of his brain were starting to click again. She'd mentioned something about her past earlier. "By the boyfriend your mother wanted you to stay with?"

She nodded, but he didn't miss the way her lips pressed together in a taut imitation of a smile, or the way her hands slipped across her belly and she hugged herself.

"Roger Campbell. He got pissed off when I refused to have sex with him. Apparently, my mother had promised him that I would. It was her solution for getting him to take me back, I suppose." Opening up a dead body never made Niall feel physically ill the way Lucy's matter-of-fact recitation of the crime against her did. "It was a shaky relationship to begin with. I didn't want to take a step I couldn't turn back from. To be honest, I didn't want to end up like Alberta—so dependent on a man to take care of her that she didn't care what it cost her." Her shoulders lifted with a weary sigh. "It cost me too much, anyway. That's why I can't have kids, you know. He broke a couple of ribs, damaged my…" She rubbed her hand across her flat belly. "I had to have emergency surgery."

Every one of Duff's rich vocabulary of curses raced through Niall's head. But only two words came out. "I'm sorry."

For a lot of things. Lucy was a natural caregiver. She should have scads of children and dozens of relatives to share her life with. That this woman should have been so used, so hurt by the people who were supposed to love her, gave him a clearer understanding of her obsession with tracking down her foster daughter and saving her. He'd redouble his efforts, as well. Maybe then she'd believe that she was not alone in her quest to do whatever was best for Tommy.

"It's not the memory, you know. It happened. Life goes on. Roger went to prison and I moved to Kansas City. But I didn't want to ever be in an ER again, feeling so useless, like there's not a single thing I can do to help myself. Especially when I know there's someone I *can* help. Someone who needs me. I want to go see Tommy and make sure he's all right. At least I could be taking care of him right now. That would be something useful I could do to help

Diana. It's important to feel useful, isn't it?" Lucy paused for a moment. "Oh. And the light-bulb just went on. I think I understand where you're coming from now." She reached for the hem of the scrub shirt. "Take your picture."

Niall curved his grip around both her hands, stopping her. She wasn't a DB on an exam table at the lab. She was a living, breathing, beautiful woman with fears and goals and needs he should be addressing instead of falling back on the procedures and science that only made him feel comfortable and in control—not necessarily better.

Her fingers trembled within his grasp, drawing his attention to her icy skin and the sea of goose bumps sweeping up both forearms. Instead of taking the photo, he put away the camera and pulled his ME's jacket from his kit. It was little more than a windbreaker with a knit cotton lining, but he slipped it over her shoulders anyway, wanting to shelter her—no, needing to protect her—from at least one thing in this world that had or could ever hurt her.

"You are the coldest woman I've ever met." When she arched a questioning eyebrow, he realized how that must have sounded. "Temperature-wise. Not personality-wise. Not at all. You know, cold hands, warm…"

"No wonder your brothers tease you. You're such a straight man, Niall." Her expression had changed from accusation to a full-blown grin, and he felt the muscles around his own mouth relaxing. "That's a wonderful compliment. Thank you." She slid her arms into the sleeves and rolled up the cuffs to expose her hands. "This does feel better. I swear, you're as warm to the touch as I am cold all the time." This time, she was the one to draw back in embarrassment.

Niall chuckled and pulled the collar of the jacket together at her neck. "It's nice to know I *can* offer something you appreciate."

She curled her fingers around his wrists, keeping them linked together. "I appreciate everything you're doing for me—for us—Diana and Tommy and me. I just need you to remember this is a team effort. You don't get to say whether or not I help. I'm going to."

"Understood. But you are a steep learning curve, woman." He dropped his forehead to rest against hers, carefully avoiding her injury. "And I just need you to understand that, in your efforts to save the world—"

"Just my little part of it."

Niall conceded the point, but not the entire negotiation. Her little part of the world seemed to be a far too dangerous one for his liking. "I need you and Tommy to stay in one piece."

Lucy tilted her green eyes beneath his, looking straight up into his probing gaze. "Speaking of Tommy—I know he's only a couple of weeks old, but I think babies can sense separation. He's already lost contact with his mother. I don't want to be gone so long that he thinks we've left him, too."

He could feel her trembling, an indication that the hospital's cold air was still affecting her. Cupping his hands over her shoulders, Niall rubbed up and down her arms, instilling what warmth he could before reluctantly raising his head and breaking contact with her. "I don't want that, either. Let's go upstairs and check in with him. I want to find out what Dad decided about Grandpa, too."

"And then we'll go to the lab?"

Niall gathered the evidence bags he'd labeled and stowed them inside his kit. "I think I'd better take you home so you can rest. You'll at least want to put on some of your own things."

A hand on his arm stopped his work. "I need answers more than I need sleep or clean clothes. I can watch Tommy, and we'll stay out of your way while you work. I have a seriously bad feeling that there's a clock ticking somewhere in Diana's life. That she doesn't have a lot of time. I need to know why she was with that man. Maybe the blood you found *will* tell us who he is. Diana said I was the only person she could count on. I need to know why she keeps running away from me instead of allowing me to help."

Taking Lucy and Tommy to the lab with him wasn't the wisest course of action. With them there it would be a challenge to focus on all the tests he needed to start running. But it was what Lucy wanted.

"Okay."

She picked up his camera and handed it to him, helping him finish packing. "Oh, and never *threaten* to kiss me again, okay, smart guy? I know relationships are a challenge for you. At least, I think that's what I'm learning about you. Don't overthink it when you're attracted to someone. If you're afraid for me or worried about Tommy or your grandfather and you have that raw feeling inside that you don't quite understand, finding a logical explanation won't make it go away. All that does is distance you from your real feelings. If you want to kiss me, go for it. Don't make it some little scientific experiment and don't do it to shut me up. Either kiss me because you think there might be a special connection between us or don't do it at all."

And with that intriguing little life lesson hanging in the air for him to analyze, Lucy walked out of the ER, leaving Niall to gather up his equipment and follow.

Chapter Seven

Answers were not to be found at the crime lab.

Lucy watched while Niall made phone calls and ran tests and accessed computers, but apparently forensic science, while it worked miracles in many ways, moved at a much slower pace than she expected. Results were coming in due time, Niall promised. But his patient attention to detail made her feel as if she was suffering from ADHD. Or perhaps, with Tommy asleep and Niall running tests and consulting with the CSIs and lab technologists in the building, while Lucy had nothing to do but pace, she only felt useless and isolated and not able to do one small thing to help find Diana. Even knitting was out of the question, since everything in her bag had gotten soaked with the rain and would need time to dry out before she could finish Tommy's cap or start any other project.

New locks for Lucy's front door couldn't be found, either, at least not until the entire door frame could be replaced. Which meant another night of sleeping on Niall's couch, fixing breakfast together, changing the dressing on her stitches, reminding Niall to put his books away and get some rest. She enjoyed a surprise visit from Duff and Keir with a pizza, loving how Niall murdered all three of them in the most competitive game of penny-ante poker she'd ever played. The next day she enjoyed the tour of Thomas Watson's big two-story house even more when they went over to help move furniture, install a ramp, and share a big pot of Millie's chili and cornbread around a long farmhouse table. She and Niall took turns feeding, diapering and playing with Tommy and wrestling him away from pseudo uncles and wannabe grandparents.

It was forty-eight hours of the family life she'd always dreamed of—and she had to constantly remind herself that it wasn't real. Lucy and Niall were just friends. Neighbors. Two concerned adults who'd joined forces to care for and protect an abandoned child.

Domestic bliss this wasn't. Not really. It hurt to discover herself feeling so at home with Niall's boisterous family, knowing all the while their laughter and friendship and support was just a temporary gift. It hurt even more to realize how easily her attraction to her handsome, geeky neighbor had grown into something deeper. She was becoming as addicted to Niall's quiet strength as Tommy was, and Niall's fierce devotion to a cause—her cause—gave her a sense of security and importance she'd never felt before.

What an idiot. She'd fallen in love with the brilliant doctor next door. And since love wasn't something that could be examined under a microscope or explained in twenty questions, she knew that Niall was sweetly clueless to the depth of her feelings for him. As for what he might feel for her? Since he scarcely acknowledged his feelings about much beyond his work and family, that was as much of a mystery as locating Diana and identifying the young man who'd threatened her in the elevator, then assaulted her when she'd refused to heed his warning. What logical benefit could she offer the inimitable Dr. Watson, anyway? Despite their friendship, Niall would probably want someone a little more staid and respectable, someone who didn't butt her nose into things and leave chaos in her wake. As much as he loved his family, he probably wanted someone who could give him that, too—lots of little shy brainiacs who would quietly change the world one day. Nothing like setting herself up for heartbreak.

So it was an easy decision to go back to work on Tuesday, returning her life to some sense of the independent normalcy she was used to. Since she and Niall worked opposite shifts, they'd agreed that she would take Tommy to the office with her. Either because he was still worried about her head injury or because he didn't want her and Tommy to be on their own and unprotected for any length of time, or some combination of both reasons, Niall insisted on driving her and the baby to her office. After dropping them off in the morning, the infant could nap comfortably in one of the family visitation rooms while she caught up on her caseload. And with Niall putting in so many extra hours at the lab and with his family, he could return home and have the day to catch up on some much-needed sleep before reporting in for his regular shift.

Lucy cradled Tommy against her shoulder, turning her nose to the unique scents of baby wash and formula burps as she sang a little ditty and danced around the tiny room, lulling him to sleep. *This* would be hard to lose, too.

It was selfish to wish Tommy was *her* son, that fate would finally be kind enough to gift her with a child she loved this much. But Diana had been her child, too, for a time, until the law and the lure of a new boyfriend and an exciting career had made it easier than it should have been to lose contact and drift apart. Lucy still loved Diana and felt that inexplicable maternal urge to protect her just as fiercely as the helpless infant in her arms.

So despite the all-too-human envy in her heart, Lucy wanted Diana to be reunited with her son and for both of them to continue to be a part of her life. She'd be the mother Tommy needed until she could lay the precious baby in his real mother's arms. That would be happiness enough for her. Lucy pressed a kiss to Tommy's soft hair as pointless tears made her eyes feel gritty. "I love you, you little munchkin," she promised. "I will always do whatever is best for you."

A soft knock on the door interrupted the mush fest. Kim, one of Lucy's coworkers, opened the door to the private room and stuck her nose inside. "Hey, Lucy, your two o'clock is here."

Lucy turned with a frown. "I didn't know I

had a two o'clock. Did Mrs. Weaver reschedule again?"

"Nope. It's a guy. I didn't recognize him. If he's a client, he's new."

"New?" Lucy instinctively hugged Tommy closer, thinking of dark-haired men wielding knives and warning her to stop caring about finding Diana. "Is he wearing a leather jacket? Does he have black hair?"

Her friend with the short straight hair and freckles laughed. "Um, no. Try tall and blond. And he looks like he could bench press my car."

"Oh, no." Lucy felt the blood drain from her head down to her toes. She didn't have to see the man to identify him. Too many phone calls begging for forgiveness these past few days practically confirmed it. Her dread was quickly replaced by a flood of anger. "Here. I need you to watch Tommy. Keep him in here, out of sight."

She handed Tommy over to the other woman and apologized when his eyes opened and he stirred into wakefulness again.

"Is something wrong?" Kim asked, adjusting her grip to hold Tommy more securely. "I didn't mean to upset you. Do you know this guy?"

"Unfortunately."

"Sorry. I already told him I'd come get you,

so he knows you're here." Kim juggled to keep hold of both the baby and the blanket Lucy had covered him with. "Otherwise I would have made up an excuse. I thought he was cute. You know, in a bad boy kind of way. Thought maybe he was a cop with news about Diana and that you'd want to see him."

Lucy caught the blanket and tossed it over the edge of the bassinet she'd set up in the small room. A smidgen of hope tried to take hold that Kim could be right, but Lucy pushed it aside. The description was too accurate to be anyone but Roger. "Never be taken in by a pretty face, Kim."

"Huh?"

Ignoring the question in her friend's tone, Lucy smoothed her skirt over the tights she wore and tilted her chin above the collar of her turtleneck before closing the door and marching down the hallway. She didn't need this visit. Not today. Not ever. But maybe Roger Campbell could put some unanswered questions to rest, and she could weed out a few of the facts regarding recent troubling events that might not have anything to do with Diana.

A fist of recognition robbed her of breath for a moment when she saw the familiar face that had once haunted her nightmares. Roger

Campbell stood from the chair where he sat beside her desk and pulled off the ball cap he wore. "Luce. It's good to see you."

The feeling wasn't mutual. His hair was ridiculously short, his face a little more care-worn than she remembered from that last day in court and a new tattoo on his forearm marked his time in prison. A black-and-blue circle beneath one eye made her think he'd had a recent run-in with someone's fist. But the playful wink from the uninjured eye reminded her he thought he was still big, bad, I-own-this-town Roger Campbell.

"Say your apology and get out here." She picked up a pen from the calendar on her desk. "Do I need to sign off on something for your parole officer? That you apologized to your victim?"

He chuckled and sat without any invitation to do so. "Luce, this isn't about my parole. This is important to me, personally. I learned a lot about earning forgiveness in prison. I've taken more anger-management courses than you can imagine. I know I hurt you. But I've made peace with what I've done, and I'll never let it happen again. I'm a different man."

Lucy tossed the pen onto her desk and propped her hands at her waist. "Yeah, well,

I'm the same woman. Damaged beyond repair because of you. I didn't want anything to do with you then, and I don't want anything to do with you now."

"Look, I know I made it so you can't have babies. I remember you testifying about that in court, so I know that's important to you. But I'm gonna make up for that."

"Make up…" The nerve. The ego. She shook her head in disbelief. "You can't."

"This is for you as much as me. You have to forgive me."

"No, I don't." When she realized the sharpness in her voice was drawing the attention of others at the sea of workstations across the room, Lucy pulled out her chair and sat. She lowered her volume if not the frostiness of her tone. "I mean, maybe I already have—there's no sense letting you have that kind of power over me. But I'll never forget. I'll never trust you. Plus, I've moved on. Falls City isn't part of my life anymore. My mother isn't. You aren't. I've made a life for myself here in Kansas City. A pretty decent one. And I don't want you to be any part of it. I don't wish you any harm, Roger. I just want you to go away."

"Stubborn as ever, aren't you, sweet thing. Is there someone else?"

"Why? Are you jealous?" She turned her chair toward him, growing a little more wary when he didn't answer. "Come on, Roger. You don't really have feelings for me. I don't even think you did back when we were dating. Those were teenage hormones running amok, your sense of entitlement and ungodly pressure from your father that made you—"

"A bastard?" He studied the ball cap he twirled between his fingers as he worked through that admission. Then his nostrils flared with a deep breath, and he nodded to the bandage on her forehead. "Does he treat you right? This guy you're with now?"

"How he treats me is none of your business. Nothing about me is any of your business." Although the relationship she was defending didn't exist, there was a tall, dark-haired ME in her heart that no one from her past would ever be allowed to malign. Lucy got up and headed toward the building's front exit. "I'll show you to the door."

She heard the chair creaking behind her as he got up to follow. "Luce, if he's hurt you, I can—"

The fact that he would dare to touch her incensed her fight-or-flight response. Lucy smacked his hand away.

She waved aside the security guard who stood at the front desk. She could deal with this. Lucy McKane could deal with anything, right? She had to. Pushing open the glass front door, she stepped outside onto the concrete stoop. The brisk wind whipped her hair across her face and cut right through her clothes to make her shiver. Maybe Roger *had* developed a conscience while serving his sentence, but alleviating any regrets he might have or assisting with the atonement he wanted to make wasn't her responsibility. "You can do nothing for me. Except leave." She crossed her arms against the chilly breeze and moved to the top of the steps leading down to the parking lot. "I want to see you get into your car and drive away."

"Look, I know guys in prison who are so obsessed with their girlfriend—or kid or wife or whatever—that they killed the very person they loved. I don't want to see that happen to you."

"You're the only man who ever beat me up and left me for dead, Roger. Goodbye."

"Look, Luce, I'm only trying to make amends." He actually thought there was something he could do to make up for robbing her of her ability to bear children? "I saw a guy lurking around your building the other night. Had words with him. I could tell he didn't belong there. I just want to know it's not him who did that to you."

Lucy's eyes widened. "You know where I live?"

"I knew where you worked, and I followed you home one day last week. I've been keeping an eye on you ever since."

And he was worried about some other guy stalking her? "Never do that again or I'll call the police."

"If it is him who hurt you, that ain't right. Look, I learned some skills in prison I'm not proud of, but if you need me to have another conversation with this guy, I can make him stop."

"Another..." Lucy grabbed the cold steel railing and leaned against it. "My life is none of your business."

He shrugged his big shoulders, apparently impervious to the wind and her outrage. "I sat outside for a few hours, hoping to catch you coming or going. I fell asleep in my car. Woke up to see you running after that guy from the other night. Thought maybe you two had had a fight. I tried to have a conversation with him. He wasn't interested in listening." Roger tapped his cheek. "That's how I got this. By the time

I was back on my feet, I saw you with that guy with the glasses and figured..."

"Wait. Go back." Lucy put up her hand to stop his rambling. "You saw him?"

"Yeah. Tall guy with glasses and no shoes. He was bookin' it across the yard."

"No. The driver of the silver car. The man I was chasing. Can you describe him?"

"Black hair. Eyes so dark they looked black, too. Cussed at me in some language I didn't understand. He's not from around here."

Wind wasn't what chilled her blood now. "Did you see a dark-haired woman with him? Younger than me?"

"No."

"Was the man injured? Did you see any blood on him?"

He shook his head. Lucy needed a better witness than Roger Campbell. Had he seen the man who'd attacked her or not?

"Can you tell me what kind of car he drove?"

This time Roger nodded, his frown suggesting that she was missing the point. "Look, he was nosing around your car before he went into the building. When he came back out, I stood up for you. At least until he pulled a knife on me. Hell, I even followed him out to Independence, until I lost him somewhere along Truman Road. You gotta give me credit for that. I'll make him go away if that's what you want."

"So you hit a guy. He hit you back. I don't need that kind of protection, Roger. I need answers. If you can't tell me anything else, tell me about the car."

He shrugged. "Silver Chevy Camaro 2LS. Recent model. Two door."

"Did you see the license plate? Do you remember it?"

"Didn't think to look. I was busy trying to get out of his way before he ran me over." Lucy was already pulling her cell phone from the pocket of her skirt when Roger reached over to squeeze her shoulder. "What kind of trouble are you in?"

She shrugged off his touch. "Nothing I need your help with. Apology accepted. Please don't try to do me any favors anymore." Maybe that silver car hadn't been racing toward her. Maybe the driver had been speeding to get away from Roger. But she'd seen that car before, and the driver must want something from her. "Go back to Falls City, Roger. Don't contact me again or I'll call the police. Just get in your car and drive away."

He considered her request for a moment, then put his black ball cap back on his nearly shaved head and trudged on down the steps. "Whatever you say. I'm just sayin' I know trouble when I see it—"

"Goodbye, Roger."

Lucy stood there to verify that one, Roger was indeed leaving, and two, that it wasn't in any silver car. Learning that Roger knew where she and Tommy were living, and that someone else, perhaps even more sinister than the bully Roger Campbell had been, also knew her home address, shook the ground under her feet. There were too many threats hiding in the fringes of her life, and thus far, she hadn't been able to pinpoint one of them. Roger hadn't given her much of a lead, but it was something.

She pulled up the numbers on her phone and called Niall.

He picked up after one ring. "Lucy?"

A single word in that deep, resonant tone shouldn't be enough to soothe her troubled heart. But it did. "Did I wake you?"

"What's wrong? Are you all right? Is Tommy?" She heard movement in the background. Was he searching for his glasses on the nightstand? Unlocking his gun from the metal box in his closet or doing whatever the man did when he thought there was an emergency?

Her mouth curved with a wry grin as she

headed back into the building. "Why do you assume that something is wrong? Am I that much of a train wreck?" When he didn't answer, Lucy paused in the lobby, the embarrassing truth heating her cheeks. She started talking, needing to fill the silence. "Okay, fine. I just had a visit from Roger Campbell."

The noises in the background stopped. "The man who put you in the hospital? The man harassing you on your answering machine at work?"

So her brainy savior had pieced all that together, too. "Yes. That's him. He wanted to apologize for hurting me."

"Do you need me there to get rid of him? A guy on parole doesn't want to see a man with a badge."

"No. I managed that myself. But thanks for asking." She hurried through the maze of desks toward the back hallway and the room where Kim was watching Tommy for her. "Besides, you're supposed to be sleeping."

"I was going over a DNA report from the lab on my laptop."

"DNA?"

"Tommy's blood sample matched the DNA we got off the screwdriver used to break into your apartment. Diana Kozlow's. She's his mother."

Lucy pushed open the door to find Kim singing a country song to Tommy. She smiled as the baby batted at her friend's moving lips, fascinated by the movement and sound. Diana loved music like that, too. Well, maybe a different genre. She was just as curious about the world around her. At least, she had been when she'd lived with Lucy. She couldn't imagine loving that little squirt any more than she already did. But her heart swelled at Niall's words. "You're not telling me anything I didn't already know."

"Yeah, well, now I know it, too. I said I'd be there at five to pick you up when you got off work. If Campbell's not a problem, why did you call me?"

To hear his voice. To let his coolly rational strength remind her that she wasn't the victim of her mother's machinations or the evils of Falls City anymore. To remind herself that she wasn't alone in her quest to find the truth— that she had an ally she could depend on without question—albeit a temporary one. But she couldn't tell him any of that. The big galoot probably wouldn't understand.

Lucy winked at Kim and quietly closed the door to finish the conversation. "I have a lead on finding Diana. Or at least on identifying the man who attacked me at the hospital."

"From Roger Campbell?"

"Yes. He...I think he was one of the men fighting outside the laundry room this past weekend. He said he's keeping me safe, making up for what he did to me." Was there any other humiliating, sordid, painful element from her past that she hadn't confessed to this good man? "Niall, I don't want *his* protection."

"I'm on my way."

NIALL DIDN'T LET Lucy out of his sight for the next five hours. The research he'd done on Roger Campbell led him to the conclusion that he didn't want the man anywhere near her, even if he could provide missing information on their investigation. Not only had the teenage Campbell kicked and beaten Lucy severely enough to break ribs and cause enough internal hemorrhaging to destroy her ovaries and necessitate the removal of her spleen—the crime for which he'd been sentenced—but he'd been involved with more aggravated assaults in prison, extending his time. Niall couldn't believe that Roger Campbell's motives now were altruistic. Too much violence, too many people who didn't value her for the unique treasure she was, had touched Lucy's life already. He couldn't allow it to touch her again. Not for Lucy's sake. Not for Tommy's. Not for his own.

Now, cocooned inside his apartment by the starry night outside, Niall watched her giving Tommy a bath in a small inclined tub in the kitchen sink. He was considering calling in sick and letting someone else take his shift at the lab because it made him crazy to think of her and Tommy alone here, having to face the threat of Roger Campbell's unwanted surveillance along with the possibility of the man who'd struck her hard enough to require stitches coming back to take his intimidation tactics to a deadlier level.

He no longer had doubts that Diana Kozlow was in serious danger. Whatever mess the young woman had gotten herself into had now touched her baby's life and Lucy's. He had no answers yet, either. And for Niall, that was equally unacceptable.

He glanced over at the clock on the stove, knowing he had to head to work in just a few minutes. But leaving behind a giggling baby with suds on his tummy and a woman with a matching dollop of bubbles on her left cheek didn't feel right. The autopsy lab was hardly the place to invite a woman and child to spend the night. And though there was a cot in his office to catch a nap during extra-long shifts, he couldn't confine them there as if they were under house arrest, either.

Keir was working on tracking down the silver car Lucy had described in detail. Duff was following up on the shooting at the church, running a long-shot check on the spent casings the CSI team had recovered in the organ loft. Maybe he could find the shop where they'd been purchased and track down the identity, or at least an image from a security camera, of the shooter. His father and Millie were busy reorganizing the house to accommodate Seamus and his wheelchair, as well as the arrival of the nurse they'd hired, Jane Boyle, and all her equipment, when the two of them moved in the following week.

Although a carpenter from the building's maintenance crew had worked on rebuilding the door frame leading into Lucy's apartment this afternoon, Niall wasn't prepared to let her move back across the hall with Tommy until the job had been completed. He wasn't ready to let her and Tommy leave, period, not when he knew she was impulsive enough to follow a lead on her own if Diana Kozlow should call. Lucy didn't seem to believe that he considered them to be a team, and that that meant they should pursue any leads together. She didn't seem to understand his need for her to stop chasing bad guys who wanted to run her down with cars or bash in her head. He didn't know how to make her understand how it upset the balance of his life when he heard things like her meeting up with the man who had once assaulted her.

He needed her here. Safe. Close enough to see and hear. Close enough to breathe in the exotic scent of her shampoo. Close enough to touch.

Decision made, Niall pushed away from the counter where he'd been leaning and picked up a diaper to cover Tommy's bare bottom as Lucy lifted him from the sink. She laid Tommy on a hooded towel and dried him while Niall anchored the diaper into place before the baby watered either one of them.

Once Lucy had Tommy swaddled in her arms, Niall reached out and brushed the smear of bubbles off her cool cheek and wiped his finger on the towel at Tommy's back. "How long do you think it'll take you to pack an overnight bag for the two of you?"

He noted the blush warming her cheek where he'd touched her, and his blood simmered with an answering heat. She tilted her eyes up to his, and Niall wondered if she knew just how many shades of moss and jade and even a hint of steel were reflected there. "Are we going somewhere?"

"I can't leave you two here alone. I'll call Dad, see if it's all right to drop you off at his place."

"You don't have to bother him. We'll be fine."

He sifted his fingers into the hair behind her ear. "*I* won't be. Too many people know how to find you now. I need to know someone I trust is keeping an eye on you around the clock." With the pad of his thumb he brushed a few wayward curls away from her temple before leaning in to press a kiss to the edge of the gauze bandage there. Tommy turned his face toward Niall's voice and wobbled against Lucy's chest, either startled or excited by him coming so close. Although he trusted Lucy to keep a sure grip on the baby, Niall splayed his hand across Tommy's back. "Easy there, munchkin."

He could feel Lucy trembling, too. Her eyes shone like emeralds beneath his scrutiny of her reaction to the simple contact. But there was nothing simple about the heat stirring inside him. Niall dipped his head a fraction of an inch and her pupils dilated, darkening her eyes. He moved even closer, and a ripple of contractions shimmered down her throat as she swallowed. Niall's heart thundered in his chest, nearly drowning out her soft gasp of anticipation that clutched at something inside him and ripped it open. Niall closed the distance between them.

Her lips parted beneath his, and he hungrily took advantage to sweep his tongue inside her mouth and lay claim to her soft heat and reaching, eager response. Niall tightened his fingers in her hair with one hand and palmed her hip with the other. He turned her, pushing her back against the counter, crowding his thighs against hers to soothe the ache swelling behind his zipper. He slipped his hand beneath the nubby wool of her sweater and clawed at the layer of cotton undershirt she wore until he could slide his fingers beneath that, too, to find the cool skin along the waist of her jeans.

Squeezing her generous curves between his hand and thighs, Niall angled her head back into the basket of his fingers and kissed her harder, deeper. His chest butted against the hug of her arms around the baby, and the earthy sensuality of mother and child ignited something protective, possessive inside him. He captured the rosy, tempting swell of Lucy's bottom lip between his own, then opened his mouth over hers again, matching each breathy sound of pleasure she uttered with a needy gasp of his own.

The coo of a baby and tiny fingers batting against his chin returned Niall to his senses. With a deep sigh that was a mix of frustration and satisfaction, he pulled his hands from her hair and clothes and moved them to the baby. He caught Lucy's lips once more, then kissed her again. Each peck was less frantic, more tender, as he eased himself through the withdrawal of ending the incendiary physical contact. Finally, he angled his hips away from hers and retreated a step, pressing the last kiss to the top of Tommy's head as the curious infant clung to the scruff of his evening beard and squiggled with excitement at the sensation, which probably tickled his sensitive palm. "You want to be in on the action, too, hmm?"

Lucy's lips were swollen and pink from the same sandpapery rasp as they curved with a shaky smile before she stepped aside and turned her back to him. She set Tommy in the bouncy seat on the counter before reaching behind her to straighten the shirt he'd untucked and smooth her purple tweed sweater down over the curvy flare of the hip that was branded into his hand. "Niall, you didn't have to do that. I'll go to Thomas's for the night. I'd love to visit with your dad and Millie again, if I won't be in the way. You don't have to persuade me with a kiss."

"Persuade?" He took her by the elbow and turned her to face him again, his eyes assessing the relatively blank expression on her face. "You said when I felt raw and unsettled inside that I could kiss you."

"I meant—"

"You said never threaten to kiss you, to just do it."

Her cheeks colored with a blush, bringing the animation he was used to seeing back into her face again. "I did say that, didn't I?" She reached up to comb her fingers through that glorious muss of hair. "I forgot for a second how well you listen. Did it help you feel better?"

"Yes." Releasing her, Niall drew in a deep breath, trying to cool the fire Lucy McKane stoked inside him. He felt as though there was something unfinished between them, and he wasn't quite sure how to verbalize it. "And no. I'm more concerned about how it made you feel. I don't want to scare you off or make you uncomfortable. But then your response is so natural, so…combustible—it feeds something inside me." He scratched his fingers through his own hair before adjusting his glasses at the temples. Her frowning eyes following his every movement didn't tell him where he was going wrong in this conversation. "I know that there are rules about men and women and…and we don't have time to explore that right now."

"You worry too much about rules and logic." She reached up to stroke the hair off his forehead. Niall felt that tender caress and her returning smile all the way down to his bones. "There are some things in this world that can't be fully explained—like a mother's bond with her child or what makes one person attracted to another. Sometimes you just need physical contact to feel better. We all do. I'm not quite sure how you manage it, but you damn sure know how to kiss, Doctor. Sweeps a girl right off her feet." He liked those words, too, and was glad he wasn't the only one left a little off-kilter each time they touched. "I just need you to understand your motives if this…attraction… develops into something more than a friendly alliance. I need you to be fully aware of what you're getting with me, so that neither one of us gets hurt."

"What I'm getting with you?" That sounded like some kind of warning. "I'm not like

Campbell. I have no intention of hurting you. I don't understand."

"I know." She touched that springy spike of hair again. "I'm not about to put words into your mouth or try to tell you what you're feeling. But if anyone can figure it out, you can." She pulled away to pick up Tommy and push him into Niall's hands. "If you'll get Tommy dressed, I'll go pack a bag for us."

The lights of the city turned streets into a foggy twilight as Niall wound his SUV through the back roads south of Kauffman and Arrowhead Stadiums until he could catch Blue Ridge Cutoff and take a straight shot to the two-story white home where he and his brothers and sister had grown up. He stepped on the brake, slowing behind the last dregs of rush-hour traffic, and waited to make a turn.

While he waited, he glanced over at Lucy in the passenger seat, nodding and drumming her fingers against the armrest in time with the tune playing through her head. Or maybe it was nervous energy. She hadn't really explained herself to his satisfaction after that kiss in the kitchen, so he couldn't be sure what ideas were going through that quirky mind of hers. She wouldn't surrender herself so completely to an embrace like that if she didn't feel something for him, would she?

Lifting his gaze to the rearview mirror, he glimpsed the royal blue knitted cap peeking above the top of the car seat, where Tommy dozed in the back. It seemed he understood the baby's needs and moods better than he did the woman beside him. Niall hated to trust what most people called instincts, but something inside him was telling him that he was on the verge of finding something—or losing it—if he couldn't figure out a better way to communicate his thoughts clearly to Lucy.

He understood right and wrong, yes and no, justice and crime. He understood fear and anger—had known both growing up when he'd lost his mother or when one of his brothers or sister had gotten hurt in the line of duty, or when he'd seen his grandfather fall at the church shooting. But this fascination with Lucy, this overwhelming urge to protect her, to find answers for her—that irrational desire to touch her and listen to her ramble and see her smile— he needed to put a name to it and understand it before he said or did one wrong thing too many and he pushed her out of his life or, God forbid, someone took her from him.

"You're staring again, Dr. Watson." She giggled and the soft sound made him smile, even though her amusement with his name continued to confuse him. "Better watch the road."

"It's a red light."

"Well, it's about to change."

Not yet, it hadn't. "Why do you find my name so funny?"

"Dr. Watson?" She was still grinning. "It's the irony. The revered Dr. Watson makes me think of the Sherlock Holmes mysteries I read in school. But you are so much more Holmes, with your intellectual prowess and manners and lack of empathy for lesser mortals like me, than you are the earthy sidekick doctor."

"Lack of empathy? I feel things."

"Of course you do. It's clear how much you love your family and your work." She glanced back over the seat. "How much you care about Tommy and making sure he has a good, safe life." By the time she turned her wistful expression to him again, the light had changed, and he had to concentrate on moving with the flow of traffic. "But you're always thinking so many steps ahead of everyone else in the room that you sometimes miss what's going on right in the moment. I always thought Dr. Watson was sort of the Everyman for Holmes.

He understood the witnesses in the cases they worked on together and, to my way of thinking, translated the world for him. You know, he took what Holmes was thinking and expressed it in a way the other characters and readers understood. In turn, he took what others said or did and helped Sherlock Holmes understand their emotions and motivations." She nestled back in her seat. "I feel like I'm Watson to your Holmes. You've got the wrong name for your character. And that's why it's funny."

Niall turned the SUV onto Forty-Third Street, organizing his thoughts before commenting. "You *do* translate the world for me. I see things differently when I see them through your eyes. I'm learning through you—things that don't come from books. I admit that I'm more comfortable talking procedure with other cops or talking about a dead body into a digital recorder than I am conversing with…"

"Real live people?" He glanced over to see her sympathetic smile and, after a moment, nodded. "Niall Watson, I think you're a little bit shy. You live in your head most of the time."

The woman was as intuitive as his mother had once been. "And you live in your heart."

Lucy's lips parted, then closed again as she

turned aside to look out the passenger window. "That gets me into trouble sometimes."

Definitely. But it also enabled her to smile often and laugh out loud and feel joy and passion and even sorrow to a degree he sometimes envied. He slowed as they neared a stop sign. "Don't ever change."

Her head whipped around to face him as his phone buzzed in his pocket. "You say the oddest things sometimes."

Niall felt himself grinning as he reached into his pocket. "Translate it, okay?"

The call was from Keir. Niall instantly put on his work face. This could be something about Grandpa Seamus or the follow-up he'd asked his brother to run on Roger Campbell and the owner of the silver Camaro. He handed the phone to Lucy. "Answer that and put it on speaker for me, will you?"

She tugged her glove off between her teeth and swiped the screen. "Hey, Keir. This is Lucy. Niall is driving right now so I'm putting you on speakerphone. Okay?"

"Hey, Lucy. Is he giving you any trouble?"

Niall cut off the teasing before she could answer. "What do you need, little brother?"

"It's work, Niall." The sudden shift in Keir's

tone indicated as much. "The lab said you're the ME on call. I've got a DB at Staab Imports over on Truman Road. It's up in the old caves in the bluffs off I-435."

"I know them. Businesses rent the old limestone quarries now for warehousing inventory or running electronic equipment." But Niall had a feeling that the underground caverns being naturally cool and practically impossible to break into had nothing to do with a dead body.

"That's the spot. And I think you'd better bring Lucy along." That put him on alert.

Lucy's gaze sought his across the front seat. "Why?" And then the color drained from her face. "Oh, God. Please tell me it's not Diana."

Niall reached over to squeeze her hand as Keir quickly reassured her. "It's not your friend. Our dead body is a Latino male. There's no ID on him. But there are a couple of things at the scene I need you to see."

Niall looked across to see her blinking away tears. "You okay with this? Crime scenes aren't pretty. I can have an officer stay with Tommy in the car."

Her grip tightened around his. "I'm okay. If I can help…"

Niall nodded and released her hand to end the call with his brother and turn the SUV around. "We're on our way."

Chapter Eight

Lucy knew she had issues with staying warm. But even with gloves, a knit cap and her sweater coat, this man-made cave cut out of the limestone bluffs rising above Truman Road was downright freezing.

"You're sure you're okay with this?" Niall asked, pulling out the squarish attaché that held his crime-scene kit and a rolled-up package that looked surprisingly as though it might have a body bag inside from the back of his SUV. He tucked the package under the arm where he held the kit before closing the back of the SUV and facing her. "It's not for the faint of heart. Not that anyone would accuse you of being that."

Lucy huddled inside her layers and shivered. "I suppose there's a joke here somewhere about this not being my first crime scene."

He squeezed her shoulder, then rubbed his hand up and down her arm, feeling her reaction to the unheated open space at the mouth of the cave where he'd parked behind two police cars and an unmarked police vehicle. His eyes narrowed, and she suspected he was trying to determine whether her trembling was from the chilly temps or nerves. She wasn't sure she had an answer for him. "I'll be right there with you, the whole time. Keir, too. If it proves to be too much for you, one of us will bring you back to the car and Tommy. I'll leave the engine running so he can stay warm." He nodded toward the compactly built detective leaning against the front fender of the SUV. "In the meantime, Hud—Detective Kramer—will keep a close eye on the baby."

Lucy glanced at the young man in a denim jacket, with work boots crossed at the ankles, chewing on a toothpick while he texted someone on his phone. "Does he know anything about infants?"

"I didn't know much about infants a week ago."

Leave it to Niall to point out the logical reason she shouldn't be worried. Detective Kramer *was* wearing a gun and badge that looked authentic enough. "Are you sure Keir trusts him?"

"They're partners. I know he does. Let's go." Niall looped his camera around his neck and nodded to the detective left to guard the infant in the backseat before heading down the stone driveway in the middle of the high cave. "Hopefully, whatever Keir wants you to identify won't take long."

Lucy hurried her pace to catch up with him. "Is it bad form for me to hold the ME's hand when he's on his way to a crime scene?"

Niall reached over and caught her fingers within his grasp. "It wouldn't matter if it was."

Lucy held on as they walked past the sliding gate that had a broken padlock dangling from one of its steel bars. Deeper inside the cave she noted a serpentine trail of conduits mounted to the squared-off walls and ceiling. Niall explained that they were used to run electricity, water, fresh air exchanges and computer lines deep under the ground to supply the offices, repair shops and storage units housed inside. Lucy had seen the openings in the bluffs several times but had never had a reason to go inside before. It surprised her to see cages and iron bars shielding the businesses after hours, just like the shops on a city street downtown.

"How far back does this go?" she asked as they turned a corner around a limestone post and entered another, wider area that had only one office front next to a pair of garage doors that were large enough to drive a semitruck through. One door stood open, and the lights shining from inside the entrance bathed the whole area in an artificial yellowish light. "Is that really a whole warehouse under the ground?"

"Feeling claustrophobic?"

"A little." She tightened her grip around his hand. He didn't protest her desire to cling to something steady and familiar as they approached the line of yellow tape strung crossways in front of the open garage door. A large commercial fan over each door helped circulate the air deeper inside the bluff. The moving air tickled her nose with a familiar scent. She sniffed again and slowed her steps. "Wait. I recognize that smell."

Then she saw the sign painted on the office window and closed garage door—Staab Imports: Mediterranean Spices & Delicacies.

Lucy stopped in her tracks. "The man in the elevator smelled like that." She supposed a man who smelled like a restaurant could also work for a company that stored and shipped the spices and ingredients a restaurant chef would use. She swiveled her gaze up to Niall. "Does your brother want me to identify the body?"

Niall's grim gaze indicated that was a likely possibility. "We'll take care of this fast and get you out of here while I work."

Lifting her chin to a resolute angle, Lucy followed the tug of Niall's hand.

Keir Watson appeared at the garage opening and lifted the yellow tape when he saw them approach. The hand he shook Niall's with was gloved in sterile blue plastic, and he winked at Lucy. "Thanks for coming. Back here." She could see the stoicism in Niall's posture and expression once he'd released her and knew he was changing from the man she was falling in love with into the city's night-shift expert on analyzing dead bodies. Keir was as efficiently businesslike as she'd ever seen him, too. He led them between two long rows of pallets piled high with bags and crates labeled Sea Salt, Rosemary and Olive Oil. "I called the ME wagon for a pickup, but I wanted you to see this first before the CSIs cleared the scene and sent the body to autopsy. The custodian who discovered the body thinks our vic might have interrupted a robbery. There's a safe in the warehouse's office, and Friday is payday, so it should have money in it. Apparently, these guys deal with a lot of immigrant and low-income labor. They prefer cash instead of maintaining bank accounts."

"But you don't think it's a robbery?" Lucy questioned.

"No, ma'am. The safe hasn't been opened. I've got a call in to the owner to unlock it for us, though, to check the contents."

"We passed the office out front," Niall pointed out. "A thief wouldn't need to enter the warehouse. This is something else." He lifted his camera and paused to take a few pictures of the footprints and scuff marks at the base of one of the pallets. "Looks like an altercation of some kind happened here." He pointed back toward the exit and then in the opposite direction into the makeshift walls of food and spices. Lucy didn't need a medical degree to see the different sizes and designs of shoe imprints in the thin layer of dusty residue on the floor. One track led to the exit while the other followed the path Keir was taking. But how did Niall know the different trails had anything to do with the crime and hadn't simply been left by the people who worked here? He pointed to the partially flattened burlap bag about chest-high in the pile. There was a small hole in one corner and a scattered mound of ground dry oregano at the base. Niall snapped a picture of the dark red stain in the material surrounding the hole. "Make sure one of the CSIs gets a numbered photo of this, and cut out that piece for analysis."

"Got it." Keir jotted the order on his notepad and ushered them on to the scene she was dreading. "I figure whatever started there ended here."

They turned a corner to meet a forklift jammed into a stack of crates filled with broken and leaking bottles.

"Watch your step," Keir warned. "The spilled oil makes the floor slick."

But shaky footing wasn't what caused Lucy to shudder and recoil into Niall's chest. A man was pinned upright between the pallet on the raised forklift and the wall of crates. He stood there, frozen forever in time, with blood pooling above his waist where the empty pallet had caught him. But even that ghastly mess wasn't the most disturbing part of the scene.

Now she understood why Keir had wanted her to come with Niall.

There was a soiled piece of fabric draped over the man's head and chest—a square of white knit cotton dotted with yellow, red and blue trucks.

The baby blanket someone had stolen off Tommy that night in the laundry room.

Keir must have put two and two together and had been waiting to see her reaction to the way the murder victim had been displayed. "So you do recognize it. I thought it matched the description you gave Niall."

Niall switched positions with her, putting his tall body between her and the bloody scene. "You didn't put Lucy through this to identify a stolen baby blanket."

Keir shook his head. "I'm sorry, Luce. The blanket wasn't the only part of this mess that was too familiar for us to ignore." He nodded to the CSI working nearby to remove the blanket and place it in an evidence bag. Keir was talking to his brother now. "This death shows a lot of rage."

"Or an act of desperation." Niall moved to keep her from seeing the dead man as the blanket was removed. "Who uses a forklift to kill a man?"

Lucy sensed where this conversation was going. "Someone who couldn't overpower him on her own?" She was already shaking her head. "Diana didn't do this."

"I need her to see him, Niall." Keir reluctantly asked his brother to step aside.

Standing like an unmoving wall in front of her, Niall explained a few practical details. "Lucy, the victim's eyes are open. His face is bruised and puffy, partly from what appears to be a fight, and partly from the initial stages of postmortem swelling as fluids disperse through the tissues. He won't look like the body of a deceased person you've seen at a funeral."

His facts prepared her, softened the jolt of him stepping aside and giving her a view of the victim's face.

Still, Lucy recoiled, maybe less from the horrible death Niall had described than from the familiar face that had haunted nearly every waking moment these past few days.

Niall stepped between her and the black-haired man in the bloodied leather jacket once more. "Is this the guy who assaulted you at Saint Luke's Hospital? He fits the description you gave Duff."

Lucy nodded. "That's him."

But the situation could only get impossibly worse. Bless his practical, protective heart, Niall couldn't shield her from the other detail that had been hidden beneath the baby blanket. She peered around his shoulder to confirm the truth.

"Please tell me I'm not imagining that." Niall

reached for her, but Lucy was already pointing at the dead man's chest. "What is happening? Why? My poor girl."

She gasped and pressed her fist to her mouth, resisting the urge to gag as the rock walls swayed around her. Niall caught her by the shoulders and backed her away from the body. He pushed her clear around the corner and leaned her up against an undamaged stack of crates. He hunched his shoulders to bring his height closer to hers, demanding she focus on him and not the scene they'd left behind. "Deep breaths, sweetheart. Deep breaths."

The endearment he used barely registered. Her mind was too full of the image of that screwdriver with plastic jewels decorating the pink handle plunged into the dead man's heart. It was the mate to the one Niall suspected had been used to break into her apartment the day Tommy had been abandoned there.

"Lucy." Niall's voice was as firm as the grip of his fingers around her chin as he tipped her face up to his. "Don't faint on me. Are you with me?"

"I have never fainted in my life. I'm not about to start now." Anger blended with shock and fear, clearing her head. She twisted her fingers into the front of Niall's jacket and clung to him. "I know what you're thinking. Diana did not do this."

"That's not what I'm thinking right now," he answered quietly.

Those piercing blue eyes revealed nothing but concern as he released her chin to brush a lock of hair off her cheek. Lucy tightened her grip on his jacket and walked right into his chest, pushing aside the camera that hung between them. "Put your arms around me, Niall. Just for a few seconds, okay? I need…"

His arms were already folding around her, anchoring her shaking body against his. His chin came to rest on the crown of her hair, surrounding her with his body. She snuggled into his heat, inhaled his scent, absorbed his strength.

Several endless moments passed until her world righted itself and she could draw in a normal breath. Niall showed no signs of letting go, and she wasn't complaining.

But the comforting embrace lasted only a few seconds longer until Keir cleared his throat beside them. "I hate to do this, you two. But the sooner we can get some questions answered, the sooner Lucy can leave. Do you think the beating or the forklift or the screwdriver killed him?"

With a reluctant nod, Lucy pushed away and tilted her eyes to Niall's. "I won't freak out again. I promise."

"I know you won't. But you stay here. You and Keir can talk and I can work while we figure this out." Niall needed one more nudge to leave her and disappear around the corner of the crime scene.

Keir's dark brows were arched in apology. "So you recognize the screwdriver?"

Lucy nodded, hugging her arms around her waist, already feeling the chill creep into her body again. "It matches the one Niall found in my apartment—from the set I gave Diana a few years back when she still lived with me."

Keir's blue eyes glanced around the corner, no doubt exchanging a pitying, skeptical look with his older brother. His suspicions were wrong. She'd said as much to Niall. She'd say it to anybody. "Diana did not do this. Maybe someone stole her toolbox. Maybe someone is framing her."

Keir pulled back the front of his sports jacket and splayed his hands at his waist, assuming a more brotherly stance, looking less like a detective interviewing a witness. "Maybe it was self-defense. It fits the warning he gave you about staying away and making things worse.

If he was hurting her, then it makes sense that she'd want to get Tommy out of the picture."

"No. She couldn't kill anyone."

Niall suddenly reappeared, holding what looked like a meat thermometer and a wallet in his blue-gloved hands. "Would you kill to defend that baby out there? Or to protect yourself from someone like Roger Campbell?"

"That's not the same. I didn't retaliate against Roger."

"You testified against him. Maybe Diana didn't think she'd be able to get away before she had that opportunity."

Keir flipped through the pages of his notepad. "Campbell's the guy from Falls City who went to prison after assaulting you?"

Lucy glared a question at Niall, not sure she wanted every sordid detail about her past shared with his family. "He's the investigator, Lucy. I deal in dead bodies, remember?" But knowledge was power in Niall's book—understanding was the way to make everything fall into place. "Campbell said he wanted to make amends with Lucy. If he knew this guy had hurt her, could he have done this to square the debt with her?"

"Murdering someone is not squaring a debt," she argued.

"You don't think the way a criminal does," Keir suggested. "I'll add him to the list of suspects we want to question." He made the notation in his book, then turned to Niall. "Find any ID on our vic yet?"

Niall opened the wallet in his hand and pulled out the driver's license to hand him. "Antony Staab." While Keir jotted down the information from the license, Niall continued his preliminary report. "Liver temp says he's been dead about eight hours. But the temperature in here would make the body cool faster, so the time of death might be closer to dinnertime."

"That would explain why no one discovered him until the night custodian reported for duty." Keir jotted down more notes. "We'll narrow down the window of opportunity to, say, 5 to 8 p.m. Don't you think that covering the face indicates a personal connection—not wanting to see a loved one's face? Possibly remorse?"

"It wasn't Diana," Lucy reiterated.

Niall had more gruesome details to report. "In addition to the contusions on his face, his knuckles are pretty scraped up. Looks like there's an older knife wound in his flank. That probably accounted for the blood trail he left at the hospital. He had it bandaged, but there weren't any stitches and signs of infection are evident."

"So this guy was dying, anyway," Keir suggested.

"Possibly. I want to check out these other injuries before I pronounce the cause of death. See what story they tell," Niall says. "Mr. Staab here put up a good fight somewhere along the way."

Lucy had a speculation of her own. "Could he have died of those other injuries? And the screwdriver is an attempt to pin his murder on Diana?"

"Like I said, I'll know more when I open him up."

The high-pitched wail of a baby crying echoed off the cavern walls. An instinctive alarm clenched low in Lucy's belly, and she spun around. When she saw the compact detective carrying Tommy and several bags over his shoulder, she hurried to meet them. "Don't let him see this."

Niall was right there beside her. "Get him out of here, Hud."

Hud Kramer halted inside the garage-door entrance. "I'm stopping right here, ma'am. Sir."

"Is something wrong?" Lucy asked, reaching for the trembling infant and turning him in to her arms. "There, there, sweetie. Mama's here…" She went silent at the slip and pressed a kiss to Tommy's soft wool cap. "Lucy's here, sweetie. What do you need?"

Tommy's little toothless mouth opened wide as he squinched up his face and cried against her ear.

"Easy, bud." Niall moved behind Lucy to catch Tommy's gaze. "You're making a lot of racket for someone your size."

Tommy's cries stuttered and he turned his head to the sound of Niall's voice. But then he cranked up again.

Hud held his hands up in surrender. "The kid started hollering. I tried to give him one of those stuffed toys, but that only helped for a few seconds. I didn't smell anything, but I didn't open him up to check, either." He pulled the diaper bag, plus Lucy's knitting bag and her purse, from his shoulder. "Not sure what the issue is, so I brought everything. I wasn't sure what you needed. Thought maybe I could be more help back here than walking him around the car over and over."

Keir had joined the group, too, and was making faces to distract Tommy, but with little success. "I thought you said you had a half dozen nieces and nephews."

His partner shook his head. "I'm the fun uncle. I play horsey with them and give them drum sets for Christmas. I don't deal with their personal issues."

"It's too cold in here for him to stay." Niall peeled off a sterile glove and caught one of Tommy's batting fists between his fingers and guided it to the infant's mouth. "Hey, munchkin. What's the sit-rep?"

The instant she heard the sucking noise around his tiny fingers, Lucy diagnosed the problem. "He's hungry."

Niall released Tommy. "He's starting to put on some weight. Maybe he needs to eat more. Or more frequently."

"Hey, Mom and Pop." Keir was grinning as he interrupted them. He thumbed over his shoulder. "Crime scene, remember?"

All too vividly. The baby whimpering around his tiny fist must be feeling as helpless and distressed as Lucy was right now. She glanced up at Niall and the other two men, glad to have something to do. "I'll take him."

"Don't go back to the car by yourself," Niall warned. "The killer could still be close by. And if Campbell's watching, I don't want him to see the two of you alone."

"Even if he's too young to know what's going on, Tommy can't stay here. We'll be fine."

"That's unacceptable."

"Niall—"

"You can use the office right next door, ma'am." Hud Kramer extended a hand toward the entrance, offering a quick compromise. "There's a restroom in there and it's unlocked. Until the owner comes to open the safe, we've eliminated it as part of the crime scene. There are enough cops around here that we'll be able to keep an eye on you and the kid."

Lucy nodded her thanks and hurried as far away from the grisly murder scene as she could get.

The bell over the door startled Lucy and set Tommy off on another crying jag. "Poor guy." Quickly assessing her surroundings, she dropped her bags on top of the gray metal desk in the center of the room and balanced the baby in one arm while she unzipped the diaper bag and pulled out the items she'd need to prepare a bottle. She was learning to juggle things with surprising efficiency, although the job would have gone a lot faster if Detective Kramer had thought to bring Tommy's carrier, too. Since everyone from KCPD seemed to have a job he or she was working on, she didn't want to ask any of them to run to the car to retrieve it. She rubbed her nose against Tommy's, distracting him for a brief moment from his hunger pangs before he cranked up again. "You and me—we can deal with anything, right?"

Once she'd warmed the formula a tad under the hot water tap in the adjoining restroom, Lucy snugged Tommy in the crook of her arm and gave him the bottle. The instant his lips closed around the tip, his crying changed to greedy little grunts of contentment. Lucy kissed away the tears on his cheeks and let him have his fill. While Tommy ate, she walked around the office, mindlessly taking in the neatly arranged awards hung on the walls, as well as the vibrant silk flowers on top of a file cabinet and bedazzled pencil holder on the desk that added a woman's touch to the otherwise austerely masculine room.

Tommy was smiling and full and playing with her hair by the time Lucy's gaze zeroed in on the familiar handwriting on the calendar beside the pencil holder. She read the lines and notation marking off several weeks in February and March. "Maternity leave."

Maternity leave? Diana's penchant for glittery objects? The handwriting? Being warned to stop looking for her by the dead man found at the same business? "This is your mama's desk."

But Niall would need concrete evidence to prove that her foster daughter had been in this room—that she had a connection to Staab Imports and one of its namesake employees, Antony Staab.

Eager to find anything that might lead her to Diana and clear the young woman of suspicion, Lucy knelt down to pull the changing pad from Tommy's diaper bag and spread it on the area rug beneath the desk. Then she pulled the needles out of her knitting bag and squished the yarn and fabric inside to create a safe spot to lay him down. Once he was content to snuggle with his stuffed toy and watch her move above him, Lucy started searching. She opened drawers and sifted through files and office supplies. She wondered about booting up the computer, but decided to save that as a last resort. Instead, she flipped through the names and numbers in an address book that revealed business associates like grocery stores and restaurants, and foreign names she couldn't pronounce. But there was no record of Diana anywhere.

She tried to open the center drawer next, but

it was locked. Remembering her long steel knitting needles, she pulled one from her purse and wedged it between the drawer and desk, twisting and jabbing until something tripped inside and she could slide the drawer open. "Victory."

Setting the needle on top of the desk, she opened it wide to find some loose change and dollar bills, along with a calculator and a tablet computer. She was about to close the drawer again when she spotted the corner of what looked like a blurry photograph poking out from beneath the tablet. But when she pulled the paper free, she discovered the torn-up squares of an ultrasound printout that had been carefully taped back together. Her gaze went straight to the numbers and letters printed at the bottom. *Baby Kozlow.* Proof.

She found another photograph underneath the mended printout. Unlike the grainy ultrasound, the image on this one was crystal clear. "Oh, no. Oh, God no."

It was a photograph of a pregnant Diana standing with the man who'd been so violently murdered in the warehouse. Antony Staab. He had his arm around her shoulders, his straight white teeth beaming against his olive skin. They were dressed up in this photo—suit and tie, maternity dress. Diana stood with her hands cradled beneath her heavy belly. But she wasn't looking at the camera. And she wasn't smiling. Was the dead man the father of her baby? Were the police right? Had Diana surrendered her baby to Lucy to keep him from this man who stole her smile? Had she killed Antony Staab in self-defense? Were those Diana's footprints that Niall had photographed at the scene of that so-called altercation?

She needed to show this to Niall and Keir. Diana worked here, maybe in past tense. But she definitely had a connection to Staab Imports. And now Niall would have a name and a whole dead body he could use to find answers. He could prove to his meticulous satisfaction that Tommy's father was the dead man in the warehouse.

Lucy stuffed the printout and photo into her purse and closed the drawer. But she jumped at the bell ringing above the door and snatched up her knitting needle as if she could defend herself with so simple a weapon.

Her racing heart stuttered a beat, and she stumbled back into the rolling chair when a stocky, black-haired man wearing jeans and a leather jacket stepped into the office. Just like the dead man.

"You… How…?"

"What are you doing in my office?" The man asked the question in a crisp foreign accent. "Who are you? Why are you going through my things?"

"Your things?" He didn't strike her as the flowers and glitz type. But she was shocked enough that she could do little more than parrot his accusatory questions.

"I know they are not yours."

How could a man be alive and dead at the same time? "Who are you?"

He advanced to the opposite edge of the desk, glanced down at the knitting needle she wielded like a sword, then looked back at her. His angular features were harsher, more lined than the quick glimpses she remembered from the hospital.

"I am Mickey Staab. Mikhail. I own this place." Did he know Diana? She'd need more proof to convince Niall, but she was certain these were her foster daughter's things. "I asked, what are you doing here? You are trespassing on private property."

Mickey, not Antony. A brother? Cousin? Her breath unlocked from her chest as a rational explanation kicked in. "I'm Lucy McKane. The police told me to wait in here." She pulled the needle down to her side and summoned her compassion. "There's a dead man in your warehouse. Niall—Dr. Watson, the medical examiner—said his name is Antony Staab. Is he a relative of yours?"

The man's predatory demeanor changed in a heartbeat. The harsh lines beside his eyes softened.

"Anton?" He collapsed in a chair on the far side of the desk. He dropped his face into his hands. He shrugged his shoulders as if in disbelief before he looked up at her again. "He is my brother. *Was* my brother."

"I'm sorry for your loss."

"Anton is dead?"

"Murdered, actually. I'm so sorry, Mr. Staab."

"Murdered? When the police came to my house about someone breaking into the warehouse, I had no idea they meant…" He signed a cross over his head and heart and muttered something in his native language. Then he pushed to his feet. "How? Who did this?"

"That's what the detectives and ME on the scene are trying to figure out."

He paced the small office twice before stopping across from her again. "You're no detective. Why are you here?"

She supposed anger was a normal response to grief, but Lucy wasn't exactly feeling her stubborn, independent self right now. She slid a step toward Tommy, feeling the need to protect as well as the need to be closer to an ally— even one only a few weeks old. "I'm a witness."

"A witness? You saw someone breaking into my warehouse?" His hands curled into fists before he pointed toward the warehouse. "You saw this...killing...happen?"

"I'm not a witness to the murder. But I met the victim. It's a long story." Lucy picked up her purse and stuck the knitting needle inside, checking on Tommy as she stooped down. His arms and legs were stretched with tension, a sure indication that he was probably filling his diaper or hungry again. *Please don't cry, munchkin.* She sent the telepathic plea before she quickly straightened. "Maybe you'd better talk to the police before I say anything I shouldn't."

"Yes, I will talk to them. I know who is responsible." He was pacing again, his cheeks ruddy with temper. "That witch. She was no good. I knew she would be trouble. I told Anton to stay away from her."

Lucy tried not to bristle too much at the insults to the woman she was almost certain was Diana. "The police think there could have been a robbery. There was certainly a fight of some kind."

"A robbery?" The pacing stopped, and he crossed to the safe behind the desk. "She knew the combination. I wouldn't put it past her—"

Tommy cried out from his makeshift bed, and Mickey Staab halted. His dark, nearly black eyes narrowed with a frown as he glanced down at her feet. "You have a baby here?"

"Yes, he's…" Tommy mewled softly, his discontent growing. When Mikhail squatted down as if to touch him, Lucy quickly bent to scoop the infant up into her arms and circle to the far side of the desk. He couldn't belittle the mother and then expect to be all coochie-coo with the child. "His name is Tommy."

"Tommy?"

"Yes."

"A boy? You have a son?" He followed them around the desk, smiling, in awe of the baby he'd discovered, it seemed.

Tommy's fussy cries grew in duration and decibels. Despite Lucy's cooing words and massaging his back, he was probably picking up on the tension she was feeling. "He's very precious to me."

"You are a lucky woman." Mickey Staab palmed the top of Tommy's head, touching without asking. Lucy cringed away. "Who is his father?"

Suddenly, a tall, stern Clark Kent wannabe filled the open doorway. "If you have any questions, you ask me." Lucy exhaled an audible gasp of relief as Niall took Tommy into his arms and angled his shoulder between her and the business owner. She wasn't even jealous that the baby calmed down at the sound of his voice. She was glad to see him, too. "I'm Dr. Niall Watson, KCPD crime lab. Are you Mr. Staab?"

Backing out of her personal space now that Niall was here, the shorter man answered. The momentary joy he'd shown at discovering a baby disappeared beneath a resigned facade. "Yes. The victim is my brother, Anton?"

"That's what his driver's license says." Niall nodded to the door. "There's a Detective Keir Watson in the warehouse. He'll need you to make a positive identification of your brother." He inclined his head toward Hud Kramer, waiting outside the door. "Detective Kramer will show you where to go."

Mickey Staab hesitated, looking at the baby before giving Niall a curt nod. "You are a lucky man." He leaned to one side to include Lucy. "And a fortunate woman. Congratulations." He was almost out the door when he paused to slide his hands into the pockets of his jacket and face them. "Do you always bring your family to the scene of a murder?"

"We're not exactly—"

Niall cut her off and motioned Hud into the room. "Detective Kramer?"

Hud's grin was friendly enough, but the broad span of his shoulders and muscular arms crossed over his chest indicated he could be very persuasive if he needed to be. "This way, Mr. Staab."

After the two men had disappeared, Niall pushed the door shut and turned Lucy in to his chest. He wrapped his arm around her, holding both her and the baby. "Hud said you were having a conversation with some man he didn't recognize, and I just needed to see that you…" His chest expanded against her cheek with a deep breath. "I thought it might be Roger Campbell paying another unwanted visit. That he'd followed you."

"I'm okay, Niall." She wound her arms around his waist and willingly snuggled close to his strength. "I needed to see you, too."

"Did Staab frighten you?"

Lucy nodded against his chest. "He's understandably upset. And normally, I could deal with that. But he looks just like his brother—like that dead man. For a minute, I thought I was seeing a ghost. The two of them could be twins."

"He's a ringer, all right." She felt his lips stirring against her hairline. "I'm sorry he scared you. Kramer shouldn't have left you alone."

"I'm better now—just hearing your voice, feeling your warmth around me…" Smiling at the fleeting sense of security this man instilled in her, Lucy reached up to touch the baby. "I'm as bad as Tommy. You have the same effect on both of us."

"It'll be another thirty minutes or so before I'm finished with the body. Do you want me to have Hud or one of the other officers drive you back to the apartment?"

"No. I don't want to be that far from you. Besides, someone has to stand up for Diana before everyone around here railroads her into a murder charge."

"There's a difference between exploring all the possibilities and—"

"Wait." Lucy pushed away, remembering her discovery from a few minutes earlier. She scooped up her purse and pulled out the wrinkled printout and photo she'd found. "Look at these. I found them inside the desk. And this is Diana's handwriting on the calendar. I think she must have worked here. And the ultrasound has to be Tommy."

"So she definitely knew Antony Staab."

"I'm sure they drove away from the hospital together in the same truck."

"You were nearly unconscious—"

"No. Look." Enough with the skepticism. She was giving him the facts he wanted. She crossed to the office's front door and pointed to the logo on the window. "This is what I saw on the side of the truck. Staab Imports. We have to find out if their company uses orange-red trucks. And you have to do that blood sample thing on the body so you can prove Antony is the father. And then we can find out who else might have wanted him dead."

"No." Nodding in that sage way of his, Niall joined her at the door and slipped the baby into her arms. "*I* have to find out. You stay here with Tommy. Lock this behind me so you don't have any more surprise guests. I'll have Keir wait to check the safe until after we leave. I'll figure out how all this connects to Diana's disappearance."

"She didn't kill Anton," Lucy insisted.

"Right now, I can't state anything conclusively. But I'm willing to work with that hypothesis."

"Niall?" Slipping her fingers behind his neck, Lucy stretched up on her toes. The moment she touched his lips, his mouth moved over hers in a firm, thorough, far too brief kiss.

"Feeling raw inside?" he asked as she dropped back onto her heels and pulled away.

Lucy smiled, wondering if the smart guy would ever figure out how much she loved him. Whoa. The rawness inside her eased as the revelation filled her. This wasn't just a crush or an alliance. This was way more than friendship or gratitude. "Not so much anymore." Still, the truth was bittersweet. She tried not to wonder if Niall was capable of comprehending that kind of love, much less whether he could ever feel that way about her. "Go. Find the truth. We'll be waiting here for you."

Chapter Nine

Lucy buttoned up a cable-knit cardigan over her jeans and T-shirt and slipped on a warm pair of socks before unwrapping her hair from the towel she'd worn since stepping out of the shower. She hung the dark blue towel up beside Niall's and picked up her wide-tooth comb to carefully pull it through her damp hair. The swelling on her head wound had gone away, although the colorful bruise and stitches in her hairline still made her think she looked a bit like a prizefighter.

She was losing track of the days since Niall had taken her in, and making herself so at home in his bathroom made her feel as though she was living out some kind of domestic dream. Or maybe it was more like living in an alternate universe with a strong, supportive man and a sweet little baby and all the extended family and security that went with it.

Because this wasn't her life. The Watsons and Tommy weren't her family. Niall wasn't her husband or fiancé or even her boyfriend.

She was the eccentric neighbor lady who talked too much and butted into other people's business and couldn't have babies of her own.

Even though her door had been repaired and her locks were secure, Lucy was reluctant to go back to her apartment. She wasn't ready to leave this fantasy life behind. But other than insisting that he wanted to keep an eye on her and Tommy until Diana was found and her link to Antony Staab had been resolved, Niall hadn't asked her to stay. Not for any personal reason.

And somehow, she suspected that blurting out her love for him would either confuse him or scare him away. There was a little part of her, too, that hoped if she never said the words out loud that the handsome cop doctor who'd righted her world time and again couldn't really break her heart when this alliance between them ended.

She watched her face contort with a big yawn. She still had a ways to go to adapt to the long, late hours Niall kept. Although she and Tommy had dozed on and off in his office down at the crime lab while he performed an autopsy on Antony Staab, she was exhausted this morning. She'd called in sick at work, blaming some lingering aftereffects of her injury for her fatigue. Perhaps it was better, though, if they remained ships that passed in the hallway or laundry room in the late hours of the night or early morning. That was the kind of advice her mother had given her.

"Don't you go givin' your heart and time to any man, Lucy, honey. Not until he puts a ring on your finger. Or you'll be paying the rest of your life."

Her mother had been talking about the financial difficulties that had motivated every decision Lucy could remember. But she was far more worried about the emotional toll it would cost her to reveal her feelings to a man who struggled to comprehend the human heart. He'd find a way to dismiss the irrationality of such feelings, or maybe he'd decide there was no logical way a quiet intellectual like him, from a tight family and a good home, could embrace a lasting relationship with a woman like her. Lucy knew that Niall was attracted to her physically—that crazy talent for kissing he had gave that away. But she had enough experience with her mother's peccadilloes to know that sexual attraction didn't equate to emotional commitment and long-term happiness. And Lucy wasn't going to settle for anything less.

Still, he was irresistible. She realized just how far gone she was on Niall Watson when she walked into the living room and found him sitting in the recliner with Tommy. The man needed a shave after his shift at the lab. His rich, dark hair stuck up in unruly spikes above his black-framed glasses. The wrinkled blue Oxford shirt that should have completed the brainy scientist look clung to broad shoulders and strong biceps in a way that was anything but nerdy. The baby was nestled securely in the crook of one arm. Tommy looked up between big blinks to the deep, drowsy timbre of Niall's voice.

"And so your daddy's name was Antony Staab." Niall ran his finger along the page inside the folder he was holding. "These pictures are markers, which is how we visually code DNA to identify people and find out if they're related. This is your code. See them side by side? These patterns show all the alleles you have in common."

Longing aside, Lucy couldn't help but grin as she picked up the empty bottle and burp rag from the table beside the recliner. "You're reading him a DNA report for a nap-time story? He can barely see colors yet."

"You said he liked hearing the sound of my voice." That she had. "Theoretically, I should be able to read him anything and it would have the same effect."

"Theoretically?"

"Practically, then. We don't have any children's books."

Truth be told, Lucy could listen to him read from a grocery list or phone book and that deep, fluid voice would make her pulse hum. "Point made, Dr. Watson." The big blinks had won. She pointed to the child snoring softly in his arms. "You put him to sleep."

Niall set the report aside and carried Tommy to his bassinet, where he gently placed him and covered him with a blanket. He rested one hand on the butt of the gun he wore holstered at his hip while Lucy looked down at the open report. "So it's true? Antony Staab is Tommy's father?" She read through the summary at the bottom of the page and studied the graphs and statistics she didn't fully understand. "Do you think Diana is all right? Or did she get hurt in that fight with Antony?"

"Somebody's hurt, based on the injuries I saw on his body. He got a few licks in on whoever attacked him. But if she's hurt, Antony Staab isn't responsible. In fact, I may be ready to rule her out as the killer."

"May be?"

"I found traces of her DNA on skin cells inside the victim's jacket."

"I thought you said you were going to rule her out as a suspect. If you found DNA, doesn't that prove that she was there? If you think she—"

"*Inside* the jacket," he emphasized. Niall crossed the room to retrieve his crime-lab jacket from the entryway closet and came back to drape it around her shoulders, to demonstrate his point.

Lucy huddled inside the jacket as she had that day in the hospital's ER. "She wore his jacket. So she was a friend —or even something more."

"But there was no evidence of her around the stab wound itself. No trace of her on him anywhere except from when she most likely wore his jacket." Niall tossed his jacket onto the sofa and put his hands up between them as if he wanted to start a fight. "If you and I were going to tussle—"

"My skin cells, hair, maybe even my blood would be all over your hands and clothing." He wiggled his fingers, urging her to come closer. "So tell me how you think you can prove she's not guilty of killing this man who once offered her his jacket."

"How big is Diana?"

"About my size. Skinnier. At least she was the last time I saw her. Why?"

Niall grabbed her hand that still held the bottle and raised it to his chest, using her to show how Antony Staab had been killed. "He was already pinned against the crates when he was stabbed. Even being injured like that, since there wasn't any momentum to drive him into the weapon—"

"As if he was lunging toward someone in a fight?" Lucy backed up a few steps and Niall moved toward her raised hand until his chest hit the bottle.

Then he stood still and pushed her hand away to show the difference in using just her forearm to strike the blow. "It would require a lot of strength to plunge that screwdriver all the way into the heart of a stationary victim who was standing upright. The wound track showed the weapon glanced off his clavicle. But there was no second strike, just one powerful thrust that tore through his heart."

Although the forensic details were so unsettling that she needed to stop the reenactment and pull away, Lucy appreciated that his evidence supported what her instincts had been telling her all along. "You don't think Diana would be strong enough to strike a blow like that?"

He followed her into the kitchen while she rinsed out Tommy's bottle and set the parts in the dish drainer. "It's not impossible, but it's unlikely—especially if she's injured."

Hugging her arms around her middle at the sudden chill she felt, Lucy went back into the living room. "I can't stand the thought of her being hurt and frightened and alone."

"You survived it." She felt the warmth of his body come up behind her as she stood over Tommy's bassinet and watched the peacefully sleeping baby. "She will, too."

She closed her eyes against the urge to lean back into his heat and strength. "I don't suppose there's anything in that report that *does* say who murdered Antony."

"Roger Campbell is still a possibility. Staab put you in the ER. He might see killing him as vindication for his crime against you. Duff took a drive down to Falls City to find him and check out his alibi." She opened her eyes when the warmth disappeared. She turned to see him thumbing through the autopsy report again. "His killer must have worn gloves. I found no transfer of skin cells or blood in the wounds. Usually there is in a fight like that."

"You scraped under my fingernails. Was there anything helpful under Antony's?"

"Environmental residue from the warehouse, and his own blood and tissue."

"I can't imagine how frightened Diana must be." Determined to focus on Niall's belief that Diana wasn't a killer, Lucy joined him, leaning her cheek against his shoulder to look at the report with him. "Would you read to me, Dr. Watson?"

"You've heard all the pertinent details. The rest is technical jargon. Oh." He set down the file and frowned down at her. "Tired? You want me to put you to sleep, too?"

"Your voice doesn't have quite that same effect on me." She reached up to brush that spiky lock of hair off his forehead and ease the concern from his expression. "But I do find it soothing."

"What do you want me to talk about?"

"It doesn't matter, really. Anything. Everything. Whatever you want so long as I get to be a part of the conversation."

He considered her answer for a moment, then

unbuckled his belt to remove his gun and holster and carry them into the bedroom, where he set them up on the closet shelf. Just when she thought he was going to ignore her request, he came back into the living room. He caught her hand and sat in the recliner, pulling her onto his lap. "I'm so sorry you have to go through this. The aftermath of violence is something I deal with every day. But this is the first time I've witnessed firsthand the emotional consequences of that violence. I think about Grandpa going down like that with a bullet..." His hands hooked behind her knees, turning her in his lap to face him and holding her there when she would have scooted to a less intimate position beside him. "At least I know he's alive and that he'll get better. I know he's not alone."

Although the sturdy trunks of his thighs and the distinctly masculine shape of him behind his zipper were warming her hip and bottom, she suspected Niall was seeking the intimacy of comfort and conversation, too, and her heart reached out to him, even as her body buzzed with awareness. "Seamus knows all of you care about him. Your family is such a blessing, Niall."

"Diana doesn't have any family but you, does she?"

Lucy shook her head. "None to speak of."

"I wish I had better answers for you. So you could at least know where she is. I hate to see you worried like this. You have such a big heart." He slipped his fingers into her hair, curling one finger, then another into the tendrils there, softly brushing them away from her stitches. He studied the way each lock twisted around his hand until his palm came to rest against her cheek and jaw, and his gaze locked onto hers. "You're not alone, Lucy. I'll stay with you and Tommy as long as you need me."

She tried to smile at the bittersweet promise. Lucy knew he was sincere and that she was lucky to have Niall in her life. But if he suspected how much she needed the sound of his voice and his strength and heat and clever mind and kisses, would he give her forever?

Tenderly stroking her fingers through that independent lock of silky hair, Lucy wished that every day of her life could include this kind of caring. Niall needed someone to translate the world for him, someone to see beyond the erudite speech and obsessive focus and teach him to recognize his kindness and passion, and allow them to be given back to him. She wanted a family like his. She needed his calming strength and the unquestioned reliability he brought to her chaotic world. She wanted this good man to be *her* good man.

His blue eyes narrowed suspiciously behind his glasses, and she realized she'd been petting him this entire time. "What are you thinking, Miss McKane?"

"How much I want you to kiss me right now."

"That's a good answer."

Lucy felt a blush warming her cheeks. "Why is that, Dr. Watson?"

"I was thinking the same thing. That I could shake this feeling that I'm missing something important and make all those unresolved questions that are nagging at me go away if I could just…" His hand stilled in her hair. "Is this what needing someone feels like?"

Lucy nodded. It was for her, at least. His grip tightened on her thigh and scalp, pulling her into his body as he leaned in and kissed her.

His lips opened urgently over hers, giving her a taste of creamy coffee when their tongues met and danced together. Lucy wound her arms around his neck and tunneled her fingers into his hair, lifting herself into the tender assault of his firm lips. The rasp of his beard stubble against her skin kindled a spark deep inside her. The smooth stroke of his tongue over those sensitized nerve endings fanned the embers into a flame. Each demand of his mouth on hers stoked the need burning inside her.

His hands moved to her waist, lifting her onto his chest as the recliner tipped back. She twisted her hips against his belt buckle to stretch out more fully on top of him. Her breasts pillowed against the hard plane of his chest, and she crawled up higher, whimpering at the friction of her nipples pebbling between them.

Niall moved his lips to her jaw, her earlobe, the sensitive bundle of nerves at the side of her neck. He pushed aside the neckline of her sweater and nibbled on her collarbone. At the same time, he slipped a hand beneath her sweater and T-shirt. He moaned some little words of victory or satisfaction or both when he found the bare skin of her back and splayed the fiery stamp of his hand there. It wasn't fair that he could slide his hand up along her spine and down beneath the waist of her jeans to squeeze her bottom when she couldn't touch bare skin. Determined to explore the same territory on him, Lucy braced a hand on his shoulder and pushed herself up, trying to get at the buttons of his shirt. One. Two. She slipped her hand inside the Oxford cloth to tickle her palm against the crisp curls of hair that dusted his chest, and her fingers teased the male nipple that stood proudly at attention. The muscles beneath her fingers jumped, and Lucy wanted more.

Niall's hand moved inside her shirt to mimic the same action. Her breast was heavy and full as he palmed her through her bra, and Lucy groaned at the frissons of heat stirring her blood from every place he touched her. He pinched the achy nub between his thumb and finger, and she realized those breathy gasps of pleasure were coming from her mouth. She wanted his soothing tongue on the tips of the breasts he explored so thoroughly, with no barriers between his greedy touch and her sensitive skin. She wanted the straining bulge inside his jeans sliding inside her, claiming her body as thoroughly as his hands and mouth had claimed the rest of her.

She sensed he wanted that, too. His hips shifted beneath hers, spreading her legs. Her knee bumped the arm of the chair. He lifted her to center her above him, but she hit the other arm and jiggled the lamp on the table beside the recliner.

"Niall…" There was no place for her to move. No room to make this happen. "Niall—"

In a quick show of strength, he righted the

recliner and pushed to his feet, palming her bottom as he commanded, "Legs. Waist. Now."

Lucy happily obliged as he caught her in his arms, locking her feet together behind his waist as he carried her into the bedroom. From the moment they left the recliner until he set her on her feet beside the bed, she got the feeling that there was a clock ticking somewhere, that the rightness of this moment with Niall might pass before she got to live out the fantasy of being loved by this man.

He seemed just as impatient to discover his passionate side, to find solace or to explore the human connection blossoming between them or whatever this was. His lips kept coming back to hers as they unbuttoned shirts and unsnapped jeans and dropped her sweater to the floor. She pushed his shirt off his shoulders and he reached for the hem of her T-shirt. He whisked the shirt off over her head and stopped, his eyes feasting so hungrily on her breasts that he didn't even have to touch her for the muscles deep inside her womb to pulse. Leaning in to touch his forehead to hers, he skimmed his hands up her arms to slide his thumbs beneath the straps of her bra. "Heaven help me. The leopard print?"

"What?"

He drew one finger along the line of the strap down to the swell of her breast and traced the curved edge of the material into her cleavage and up over the other eager breast, eliciting a sea of goose bumps across her skin. "I've made a very unscientific study on the design and color of underwear that goes through your laundry every week."

His deep, ragged breaths blew warm puffs of air across her skin, and she felt each breath like a physical touch. If he'd been a different man, she'd have thought he was toying with her. But Niall was Niall, and she half suspected that the way he studied her body and analyzed her reactions was part of the arousal process for him.

Lucy tried to capture a rational thought for his sake. "That's a little voyeuristic."

His finger slipped inside a leopard-print cup and the back of his knuckle brushed across the sensitive pearl. Lucy gasped at the bolt of pure longing that arced from that touch to the damp heat between her thighs. She swayed on unsteady feet and braced her hands against his warm chest. "So you like these?"

"Yes. Very much. Take them off."

Lucy laughed at the growly command, loving the rare revelation of impulsive need. As he pushed the straps off her shoulders, she reached for the waistband of his briefs. "You take yours off."

And then it was a race to strip off their remaining clothes and tumble onto the bed together. She giggled at the way his glasses fogged between them when they kissed and reached up to pull them from his nose and set them gently on the nightstand.

His hand was there along with hers, pulling open the drawer and digging around inside, blindly searching while panting against her mouth. "Condom. Need to find a condom."

Lucy pushed him back onto the pillows and straddled his hips, reaching for his eager flesh, ready to be with him completely. "No need. Can't make babies, remember?"

He prodded her opening with a needy groan, but his hands squeezed her thighs, keeping her from settling over him. "That's not fair. You deserve a dozen of them."

"Fair? Maybe not. But that's life. And I'm not letting what's happened to me stop me from living this moment with you. Right here. Right now. I need you, Niall. Inside me. All around me. Setting me on fire with all that body heat."

"Technically, it's your own body heat that's rising and making it—"

"Niall?" She leaned over him, pressing a finger to his lips to shush him.

"Yes?"

"Now is when you need to stop talking. Do you want this to happen?"

He nodded.

"Then kiss me like you mean it."

"I'll do my best." And, oh, his best was crazy wonderful. He rolled her onto her back and moved between her legs, his strong thighs nudging hers apart. His hands fisted in her hair as he slowly pushed his way into her weeping core until they were completely one. He suckled on a tender breast, then stretched the hard weight of his body over hers to reclaim her mouth as he moved inside her.

As his thrusts came faster, more powerfully, Lucy gave herself over to the exquisite pressure building inside her. What he'd denied her a moment earlier, he gave back with generous attention to detail, sliding his thumb between them to the spot where they were tightly linked, bringing her right to the edge and taking her over in a rush of feverish pleasure that washed over her arching body like waves of blissful fire. And while the aftershocks were still pulsing deep inside her, Niall's body tightened over hers. With a groan of pure satisfaction humming against her throat, he released himself inside her.

By the time Lucy came to her senses and her thumping heart settled into a steady beat against Niall's, she was already falling asleep. With her head nestled against the pillow of his shoulder, he pulled the covers over them both. There were no tender words exchanged, no questions asked, no promises made. But it felt as though the man she loved wasn't going anywhere. For a few minutes on an overcast day at the end of February, when the rest of her world was in complete limbo, Lucy felt as though she was a part of something, as if she belonged.

Treasuring the gift of these precious moments together, she snuggled into the circle of Niall's arms, surrounded by his heat, shielded by his strength and saved—for a few minutes, at least—from the fears and vulnerability and loneliness she'd lived with for far too long.

LUCY WOKE UP to the distant sound of chimes playing.

She was drowsy with contentment and deliciously warm in the cocoon of the bed and the furnace spooning behind her. Only half-alert to the sunshine filtering through the blinds at Niall's window, she savored the scent of Niall's soap clinging to the cotton sheets and the earthier scent of the man himself filling her senses. She wanted nothing more than to snuggle in beneath the possessive weight of Niall's arm and leg draped across her waist and thighs.

But moment by moment, the reality of the outside world stole the dream of her blissful morning away from her.

The sun was too bright. It must be afternoon already. She heard Tommy fussing in the other room—not crying yet, but awake and realizing he was hungry or wet or alone. She heard the beep of her phone. Missed call. Then the chimes sounded again.

Lucy pushed Niall's arm aside and sat bolt upright. "My phone."

He was awake, too, tucking the covers around her naked body before swinging his legs off the side of the bed. He stood in all his lean, lanky glory, reaching for his glasses and slipping them on. "Living room. I'll get it."

"No, thanks. I can…" Ignoring her body's traitorous rush of interest in the gallant ME's bare backside, she scrambled off her side of the bed, gasping as the chill of the air hit her warm skin. Lucy crossed her arms over her breasts and shivered. She made a quick search for her clothes and grabbed the first thing she saw—

Niall's shirt that she'd tossed over the foot of the bed earlier. Feeling an increasing sense of urgency with every chime of the phone, she slid her arms into the long sleeves and hooked a couple of buttons as she hurried out the door. "Stay put. I'll get it. I need to check on Tommy, anyway."

But he was right behind her moments later in unsnapped jeans and miles of bare chest when she pulled her phone from her purse. He nudged her aside. "You talk. I've got the munchkin."

Lucy didn't recognize the number on her phone. But too much had happened in the past week for her to take the chance on ignoring it. "Hello?"

"Lucy?"

"Diana? Thank God." She braced a hand on Niall's arm to steady herself as relief overwhelmed her. "Are you all right? Are you someplace safe? I know you used to work at Staab Imports. You didn't have anything to do with that horrible murder, did you? I told the police you couldn't have."

"Even though it was my screwdriver stuck in his chest?" Diana sniffled a noisy breath, as if she was fighting back tears. "I'm so sorry to get you involved in this mess. Everything is so screwed up. I need to ask one more favor of…"

She hesitated as the baby wrinkled up his face and cried out in earnest when Niall left him lying in the bassinet to eavesdrop on the call. "Is that Dorian? He sounds healthy. Is he?"

"Dorian?"

Diana sniffed again. "Of course. Anton said you were calling him Tommy. I like it. I named him after the lead singer in one of my favorite rock bands. But Tommy's a good name. It makes him sound like a regular, normal kid. And I want that for him—"

The conversation ended with an abrupt gasp. "Diana? Yes. He's healthy. I took him to a pediatrician. Are you still there—"

A different voice cut Lucy off. "I want to hear my son."

The voice sounded familiar. It was thickly accented, deep pitched, and it could have been melodic—if it weren't for the absolute chill she heard behind the tone.

"Who is this?" she asked.

Niall's calming, more familiar voice whispered beside her ear. "Put it on speaker. Keep him talking."

She nodded her understanding and watched as he took a few steps away to call his brother Keir and order a trace on the incoming call.

"Tell me who you are," she demanded. "What have you done to Diana?"

"She does not matter" came the smug answer that frightened, angered and saddened her at the same time. "I am the boy's father."

Niall had evidence to the contrary. Lucy had seen it. "She matters. His father is Antony Staab. And he's dead."

"You lie!" Lucy jerked at the angry voice, flashing back for a split second to the night she'd said no to Roger Campbell.

But Niall's blue eyes, demanding she focus on the call and stay in the moment with him, gave her something to concentrate on. "I saw his dead body," she explained. "I read the medical examiner's report." She hardened herself against the man's curses and Diana's pleas muttering in the background. "I'm guessing you had something to do with his murder. And you tried to pin it on Diana."

Blowing off the accusation she'd just made, the man came back on the line, speaking in a deceptively calm voice. "My son was taken from me. You kidnapped him."

"No. I'm watching him for his mother." Poor Tommy's cries quieted to a mewling sound of frustration when she reached into the bassinet and captured one of his little fists in her fingers and moved it to his mouth to suckle on. "I'm his legal guardian."

"I am his father! He belongs to me. Let me hear him."

She heard Keir's voice coming from Niall's phone. "We got a ping on her phone from a cell tower downtown."

"Narrow it down, little brother. I need an exact location." To Lucy, Niall gave her the sign to draw out the conversation for as long as she could.

Lucy nodded.

"Here." She pulled Tommy's fist from his mouth and the baby wailed. Lucy put her phone next to the crying baby for several seconds before pulling it back to speak. "Is that what you wanted to hear? I need to change and feed him. Are you willing to do that kind of work to take care of an infant? To be responsible like a real father? Or is he just some prize to you? Now either tell me who you are or put Diana back on the phone." There was a terse command about explaining things and a sharp smack of sound. "Diana? If you hurt her…"

"It's me, Luce. I'm okay." But she wasn't. Diana was crying again. No wonder her foster daughter had wanted to get her baby away from such a dangerous situation. But why wouldn't she save herself, as well? "I thought after I had the baby I could disappear on the streets the way I used to before I came to live with you. You know, when I was a runaway. But I've never met anyone like Mickey before."

"Mickey?" Now the accent made sense. "Mickey Staab?"

"Yes." Diana's voice was rough with tears. "I used to cut his hair, you know. That's how we met. I thought he was handsome and charming. He offered me a job that paid three times what I was making. I thought we were going to live happily ever after. Then I got pregnant and everything changed."

Lucy glanced over at the bassinet. "All he wanted was the baby."

Diana sniffled an agreement and continued. "It's some cultural thing from his country— something about firstborn sons being raised by their fathers. But I couldn't let my baby grow up like that—with all the violence and no regard for others. You taught me how children should be treated. How I should be treated." Niall had crossed the room, pinning down some important piece of information with his brother he didn't want anyone to overhear. "He found me. He found us. I was desperate to save Dorian—er, Tommy. And then Anton, sweet,

sweet Anton, tried to help me get away. Stupid me. I fell in love with the wrong brother. I wanted to tell you that I didn't kill him. In case we don't get a chance to talk later."

How long did she have to listen to these horrible things Diana had had to deal with before KCPD could find her location and get her out of there? "What do you mean? We will see each other again. I promise you."

Guilt and regret shook in Diana's voice. "Mickey knows I left Tommy at your place. He followed Anton and me to your place the other night and tried to take him from you."

"In the laundry room."

"Keir?" Niall prompted, returning to her side to squeeze her hand. Lucy held on just as tightly.

"Yes. I wanted to see my baby one more time and explain everything to you. But this guy showed up and made everything worse." *Roger Campbell.* "Mickey blamed Anton—said his brother should be helping him get his son back, not helping…" She didn't need to explain whatever crude word Mickey had called her. "He was so angry. There was a horrible fight."

The blood at the hospital. He'd cut his own brother. Mickey Staab was a sick, obsessive man.

And now, without Antony Staab alive to

even try to protect her, Diana was completely at his mercy.

Mickey's cruel tone at the other end of the call confirmed as much. "Tell her what I said. Tell her!"

Diana's next words came out in a panicked rush. "Stay away, Lucy. You stay away and don't let my baby anywhere near—"

Lucy heard the sting of a slap and a sharp cry of pain.

Her knees nearly buckled at the helpless rage surging through her. "Diana! You sorry SOB. You keep your hands off her. Diana!"

Niall's arm snaked around her waist, pulling her to his side. She tilted her gaze to his and he nodded. Keir had pinpointed the source of the call and dispatched every available unit to the location. "We're coming for you, Staab."

For a moment, there was only silence at the other end of the line. And then, "You think you have it all figured out, Dr. Smart Cop?"

"I know you killed your brother." Niall's articulate voice held none of its mesmerizing warmth. "It's the only answer that makes sense, Mikhail. Or should I say Mickey? You and Antony are twins. That's why all the DNA at the crime scene showed up as his. You share the same genetic code. That's why I thought he was Tommy's father."

"His name is Dorian," Mickey corrected, his articulation slipping each time his anger flared. "My son's name is Dorian."

"No court of law is ever going to let you be his father. *I* won't let you be his father," Niall warned. "Now let Diana go when the police arrive, and maybe you'll live long enough for Tommy to visit you in prison someday."

"You cannot deny me what is mine." Lucy collapsed against Niall's strength at the frightened yelp she heard in the background. "The time for conversation is over. Listen very carefully, Miss McKane. I will leave the phone here so all your police friends can find it. But you—and you alone—will bring my son to me at the address I will tell you, and then I will give you this piece of trash you value so highly. If I see any police, Diana will die. If you are a minute late, she will die. If you do not bring me Dorian, you both will die."

Chapter Ten

"Is that the clearest picture we can get?"

Lucy heard Niall's voice over the device in her ear, taking some comfort in the knowledge that he was with her, even if he was stuck in a surveillance van with Keir nearly half a block away on the far side of the Saint Luke's Hospital parking lot. Meanwhile, she was making a grand show of unpacking a stroller and diaper bag from the trunk of her car, taking her time to assemble and stow Tommy's belongings before she retrieved the doll dressed in Tommy's clothing from the carrier in the backseat.

The deception was risky, but no way was she going to let Tommy anywhere near his father, especially after Mickey had murdered the baby's uncle and kidnapped his mother. While she followed the rest of Mickey Staab's directions to the letter, Tommy was safely hidden away at Thomas Watson's house, with Niall's father and Millie Leighter keeping a careful watch over the infant.

"I've got tech working on it," Keir assured him. "And remember, I've got men stationed all around the hospital complex. If Staab's Camaro or anyone matching his description shows up, we're going to know about it long before he gets to Lucy." Then she realized Keir was talking to her. "Luce, we've got you on screen. I need you to do an audio check, too."

She pulled her knitting bag out, keeping appearances as normal as possible. "Make sure you're getting my best side."

"This isn't the time to joke," Niall warned. "You know how easy it is for this meeting to go sideways. No matter how prepared we are, we can't control all the parameters. Staab is vicious and unpredictable."

"I know, Niall," she answered, wondering if he even realized how worried he was about her, and wishing she knew how to help him recognize and deal with those burgeoning emotions. "Trust me, I know."

She'd stood up to Roger Campbell in a courtroom over a decade ago, and she hadn't had backup of any kind then beyond her attorney. Today she was standing up to another violent man—but this time she had Niall Watson, the rest of the Watson clan and a good chunk of the Kansas City Police Department supporting her. Meeting Mickey Staab face-to-face again would be far more dangerous than testifying against Roger had been, but knowing she had people she could rely on in her corner this time made it easier somehow.

Niall's brother, on the other hand, appreciated a little sarcasm to lighten the tension of the situation. "We're reading you loud and clear, Lucy. We'll keep you posted as soon as we spot our guy. Are you sure you're still up for this?"

Keir, who'd worked sting operations like this before, suggested Staab had picked the parking lot at Saint Luke's Hospital because of the easy access to traffic, enabling a quick getaway once the hostage exchange was made, and because there were so many innocent bystanders around the busy public hospital who could get caught in the potential line of fire that he rightly assumed the police wouldn't be eager to get into any kind of gun battle with him. And if they cleared the area, then Staab would immediately know they were waiting for him. That left Lucy out there, unprotected and alone to face off against a kidnapper and killer.

"I'm sure." She held her breath as a car

backed out of a parking space a few stalls away. She didn't breathe again until it drove past and turned toward the hospital building. No threat there. "But I want to move to a house with a private driveway. I'm sick of parking lots."

Niall surprised her by responding to her nervous prattle. "When this is all said and done, I'll take you to Mackinac Island, Michigan, where they don't have any cars or parking lots."

Lucy looped her knitting bag over her shoulder with her purse and closed the trunk lid. "Is that an invitation, Dr. Watson?"

She didn't giggle when she said his name this time.

He didn't answer the question, either. "Let's get through the next few minutes first."

Right. That would be the smart thing to do. She checked her watch and moved to the back passenger door, unable to delay the inevitable any longer. "And you're sure you've got Roger Campbell out of the picture? I don't want him thinking he's going to come in and save the day and wind up getting someone killed instead."

Niall answered. "Not to worry. Campbell violated his parole six ways to Sunday by showing up at your office and our building. Duff's got him down at the precinct offices now booking him."

That was one less random factor about this whole setup she could eliminate. "So it's just Mickey Staab we have to worry about."

"Theoretically."

"Theoretically?" Lucy shook her head, unstrapping the doll and covering its face with the blanket she'd wrapped around it. "Is there some other bad guy you want to tell me about?"

But someone on Keir's team had spotted the car. "Be advised. We've got Staab in a silver Camaro approaching your position from the north entrance."

Lucy inhaled a deep breath, spying the all-too-familiar car turning down the lane where she was parked. She was shivering from the inside out. She was scared. Scared for herself and scared for Diana. But she wasn't alone, right? She didn't have to do this alone. "Talk to me, Niall. I need to hear your voice right now. Ask me a question or something."

"We need to talk about what happened this morning."

"What?" This morning? Did he mean making love? Or going over Antony Staab's autopsy report and DNA tests? Or something else entirely? Those weren't exactly topics that she wanted to get mixed up, especially over an open com line where Keir and a bunch of other cops could hear. "I can't talk about that right now. I can't..."

Mickey Staab's car slowed, and Lucy carried the camouflaged doll in her arms to the back of the car. The man who'd terrorized her foster daughter was close enough that she could see his dark eyes. But she didn't spot anyone else in the car with him. "Where's Diana?" she whispered, more afraid of what she didn't see than what she did.

"All right, people, this is it," Keir announced. "Eyes sharp. Nobody moves until I... Niall? Where are you going, bro? Son of..." Keir swore something pithy in her earbud. She heard a metallic slam in the distance. "Be advised. Hold your positions until I give the go to move in. We need eyes on the hostage."

Lucy adjusted the straps of her bags on her shoulders and hugged the doll to her chest as the silver car that had nearly run her down once before stopped in the driving lane only a few feet away. She swallowed hard, steeling herself for the coming confrontation. Mickey shifted the car into Park but left the engine running. She was confused when he leaned across the front seat. Why wasn't he getting out? Did he know there were a dozen cops watching him?

Eyes on the hostage. She couldn't see Diana.

"Where's Diana?" she shouted. She dipped her head to kiss the doll's forehead, keeping her eyes trained on the black-haired driver. "I did what you said. I brought Tommy. Where is she?"

The passenger door opened and a young woman tumbled out onto the asphalt with a barely audible moan.

"Diana!" Lucy lurched forward.

She froze when she saw the bloody knife in Mickey's hand. It was a long, wicked-looking thing like the one his brother had carried. Maybe it was even the same blade the monster had taken off his brother's dead body. Mickey followed Diana out the same door, standing over her as she curled into a fetal position, but crouching low enough that the door and frame of the car protected him from the eyes of any cop who might take a shot at him. He knew this was a setup. He knew he was being targeted. But he was that desperate to be united with his son.

And a desperate man was a dangerous one.

"In my home country, women are good for two things. Betraying me is not one of them."

Lucy's eyes burned with tears. "You lousy son of a—"

He pointed the knife at Lucy. "Give me my son."

Lucy inched around the hood of his car, trying to get a clear look at how badly Diana was injured. "Let me help her. Please. Let me get her inside to the ER."

His dark eyes tracked her movement until she came one step too close. He thrust the knife in her direction, warning her to stop. "My son first."

The charade had gone on long enough.

"Here he is." Lucy tossed him the fake baby and grabbed Diana's hand to drag her from beneath the open door.

Even though he was startled enough to catch the doll dressed in Tommy's clothes, as soon as Lucy threw the package, Staab must have guessed the deception. "You bitch!" He dropped the doll and charged around the door into the open.

Lucy heard a chorus of *"Go! Go! Go!"* in her ear and dropped Diana's hand to reach into her bag as he raised the knife to attack.

"You are all lying—"

She jabbed the knitting needle into his arm as hard as she could, ripping open a chunk of skin. But she'd only deflected the blade, and his momentum carried the screaming man into her, knocking her to the ground. Lucy ignored the pain splintering through her shoulder and rolled.

"Move in! Move in!" She was hearing real voices now, echoing the shouts in her ear.

Lucy was on her feet first, but she stumbled over Diana's body before she could get away. Mickey's feet were surer, his stride longer. He latched onto a handful of her hair and jerked her back. A million pinpricks burned like fire across her scalp. That knife was so very close, and help was so very far away.

Lucy heard three loud bangs.

Mickey's grip on her hair went slack, and she dropped to her knees. His dark eyes glanced up to some unseen point behind her. Three spots of crimson bloomed at the front of his jacket, and he fell to the ground, dead.

Lucy scooted away before he landed on her and turned to see Niall holding a gun not ten feet away. His feet were braced apart on the pavement. A wisp of smoke spiraled from the end of the barrel, and she looked beyond the weapon to his steely blue glare.

She'd defy anyone to spy one trace of the nerdy scientist now.

But the heroic impression was fleeting. Niall was already holstering his gun and kicking Mickey Staab's knife away from the dead man's hand as Keir and several other police officers swarmed in.

He didn't say a word but knelt beside her, switching from cop to doctor mode before she could utter a thank-you or ask why he wasn't back in the van where he was supposed to be. He checked her eyes and ran his hands up and down her arms. She winced when he touched the bruise on her shoulder, but the sharp pain woke her from her stupor. "I'm okay." She turned his hands to Diana. "Help her."

"I need a med kit!" Niall yelled the moment he rolled Diana onto her back. She was bleeding from the cut across her belly that Mickey had no doubt inflicted upon her. "Diana?" He peeled off his ME jacket and wadded it up against the gaping wound. "Diana. I'm a doctor. Open your eyes."

Lucy crawled to the other side of her and took her hand, squeezing it between both of hers. "Diana, please, sweetie. It's Lucy. Listen to Niall. Open your eyes if you can."

Diana groaned and blinked her eyes open. But they were dull and unfocused. "Luce?" she slurred through a split lip.

"Yes. It's me. You're safe now. You're safe."

"Tell me…about…my baby." Her breath railed in her chest. "Mickey…he can't end up like Mickey."

Lucy glanced over at Niall, who was doing his best to stanch the wound. When he shook his head, the first tear squeezed between her eyelashes.

She kissed her foster daughter's hand. "He won't. Tommy's fine. Dorian, I mean. He's such a good little boy. Such a healthy eater. And loud. But he's safe. You did it, Diana. You protected your little boy. You kept him safe."

Diana's eyes drifted shut again. But her swollen lip curved into a smile. "Tommy's a good name. Tell him how much I loved him."

"Diana—"

"Tell him."

"I will, sweetie. I will. I promise that he will always know what you did for him."

"I knew you'd have my back." Diana's hand grew heavy in Lucy's grasp. "He couldn't have a better mother than you. Because you were always a mother to me."

"Diana?"

Lucy knew the moment she lost Diana forever. She gently set Diana's hand on her still chest and brushed the dark hair off her forehead to press a kiss there. The rest of the world blurred through her tears—the police, the EMTs on the scene taking over for Niall in a futile effort to revive the dead woman, the cars, everything. A merciless fist squeezed the air out of her chest, and then she was sobbing.

A soothing, deep-pitched voice reached her ears. "Sweetheart, stop."

She knew very little of what happened over the next few minutes, only that Niall's arms were around her. She didn't care about the blood on his hands that were now in her hair. She didn't care about the weeping spectacle she was making of herself. The only thing that mattered was that Niall was here.

Lucy McKane could deal with anything. But not this. Without Niall, she knew she absolutely couldn't deal with this.

LUCY CRIED A lot over the next few days, a sight that tore Niall up inside every time he saw those red-rimmed eyes and felt the sobs shaking her body.

She'd lost someone she considered a daughter. She'd relived the nightmare that could have been her a decade ago if she hadn't fought and scrapped and kept moving forward with her life. Lucy talked about feeling guilty for losing touch with someone she'd once been so close to and how angry she was that she hadn't been able to find Diana in time to save her.

But Lucy McKane was a kind of strong that Niall had never known before. Yes, she cried. But she also teased his brothers and had long talks with Millie and traded hugs with his father. She was even finding things in common with Niall's sister, now that Liv and Gabe were home from their honeymoon. She laughed with Tommy when he was awake and hummed with contentment when he fell asleep in her arms.

It was an emotional roller-coaster ride that Niall wasn't sure how to help with. But he could offer practical assistance and muscle. He'd stood by her side at Diana's funeral, and now he was helping her move Tommy and her stuff back to her apartment.

He'd almost been too late that afternoon when she'd faced down a killer. He'd felt too far away watching her on a TV screen from a distant van. And though firing his weapon wasn't his first duty as a cop, it had been the only duty that day that had mattered. Mickey Staab was hurting the woman who was more important to him than any other since his mother had died. When he'd raised that knife to gut Lucy the way he had Diana Kozlow, Niall had quickly taken aim and stopped him.

And now, as he set down the bassinet in her bedroom, Niall felt as if time was ticking away from him again, as if living just across the hall from Lucy and Tommy would be too far away. And if he didn't do something about it now, he might lose them forever.

He turned to watch Lucy leaning over the changing table to rub noses with Tommy. She smiled and the baby laughed. After tossing the soiled diaper she'd changed into the disposal bin, she carried him to the bassinet and laid him inside with one of his stuffed toys.

Why did having his own space back, and getting his world back to its predictable routine, feel as though Lucy was leaving him? And why did an irrational thought like that make his chest ache?

He was memorizing the curve of her backside in a pair of jeans when she straightened and faced him. "You're staring again, Niall."

"Am I?" His gaze dropped to the rich green color of her eyes. There was still sadness there, but a shining light, as well, that he couldn't look away from.

"You don't know when you're doing that?" She nudged him out into the hallway and closed the door behind them so Tommy could nap. "I feel like a specimen under a microscope."

"Sorry. I guess I'm a little brainless when I'm around you."

"Brainless? You? Never."

He followed her out to the living room. "There's no logic to it. I can't think straight. I'm disorganized. I can't focus on my work. All I do is react and feel."

"Feeling isn't a bad thing, Niall. What do you feel?"

He raked his fingers through his hair and shook his head, searching for the definitive answer. "Off-kilter. Out of sorts. Like I never want to let either of you out of my arms or out of my sight. I think about you when we're apart. I anticipate when I'll see you again. I'm thinking of Tommy's future and whether or not he'll go to college and how he shouldn't grow up without a mother. I worry that you're not safe or that you're talking some other man's ear off or—"

Lucy shushed him with her finger over his lips and offered him the sweetest smile he'd seen in days. "I love you, too."

"Yeah." He nodded as his heart cracked open inside him and understanding dawned. "Yes. I love you." He tunneled his fingers into her hair and tipped her head back to capture her beautiful mouth in a kiss. Her arms circled his waist, and he pulled her body into his as that eager awareness ignited between them.

Sometime later, when she was curled up in his lap on her couch and he could think clearly again, Niall spoke the new discoveries in his heart. "Lucy McKane, I have a question for you."

She brushed aside the hair that stuck out over his forehead. "You know I love to listen to you talk."

"I'm a patient man, and I'll give you all the time you need."

"To do what?"

"Will you marry me? Can we adopt Tommy together after the six-month waiting period? Can we be a family?"

She grinned. "That's three questions, Dr. Watson."

"See? Completely brainless. I'm new at all this touchy-feely stuff, so be kind. Don't make me beg for an answer."

She tilted her mouth to meet his kiss. "Yes. Yes. And yes."

Epilogue

The unhappy man skimmed through the article he'd already read a dozen times before folding the newspaper and setting it on the corner of his desk. "The *Journal* says that Niall Watson was involved with a shooting outside Saint Luke's Hospital. Internal Affairs vindicated it as necessary force to protect the intended victim. It's not front-page news, but the story is long enough to mention his grandfather being well enough to leave the hospital and move home to continue his recovery."

The man sitting across from him refused to apologize if that was what this late-night meeting was about. "I did what you asked. I ruined the wedding. I got those Watson boys and their daddy all up in arms without any clue about what's going on. And there's no way they can trace anything about that shooting back to you.

For all they know, some crazy guy went off his rocker."

"Seamus Watson is supposed to be dead." He pulled open the top right drawer of his desk and fingered the loaded gun he kept there. "When I hire you to do a job, I can't afford to have you fail."

"Then tell me what I can do to make things right. Reputation is everything in my business. The next job will be on the house."

Satisfied, for the moment, with that arrangement, the man pushed the drawer shut. His employee could live for another day.

The Watson family might not be so lucky.

* * * * *

Keep an eye out for Keir's story when the next thrilling installment in Julie Miller's THE PRECINCT: BACHELORS IN BLUE *miniseries becomes available. You'll be able to find it wherever Harlequin Intrigue books are sold!*

LARGER-PRINT
BOOKS!

HARLEQUIN

Presents®

PASSION
GUARANTEED
SEDUCTION

GET 2 FREE LARGER-PRINT
NOVELS PLUS 2 FREE GIFTS!

YES! Please send me 2 FREE LARGER-PRINT Harlequin Presents® novels and my 2 FREE gifts (gifts are worth about $10). After receiving them, if I don't wish to receive any more books, I can return the shipping statement marked "cancel." If I don't cancel, I will receive 6 brand-new novels every month and be billed just $5.30 per book in the U.S. or $5.74 per book in Canada. That's a saving of at least 12% off the cover price! It's quite a bargain! Shipping and handling is just 50¢ per book in the U.S. and 75¢ per book in Canada.* I understand that accepting the 2 free books and gifts places me under no obligation to buy anything. I can always return a shipment and cancel at any time. Even if I never buy another book, the two free books and gifts are mine to keep forever.

176/376 HDN GHVY

Name	(PLEASE PRINT)	
Address		Apt. #
City	State/Prov.	Zip/Postal Code

Signature (if under 18, a parent or guardian must sign)

Mail to the **Reader Service:**
IN U.S.A.: P.O. Box 1867, Buffalo, NY 14240-1867
IN CANADA: P.O. Box 609, Fort Erie, Ontario L2A 5X3

**Are you a subscriber to Harlequin Presents® books
and want to receive the larger-print edition?
Call 1-800-873-8635 today or visit us at www.ReaderService.com.**

* Terms and prices subject to change without notice. Prices do not include applicable taxes. Sales tax applicable in N.Y. Canadian residents will be charged applicable taxes. Offer not valid in Quebec. This offer is limited to one order per household. Not valid for current subscribers to Harlequin Presents Larger-Print books. All orders subject to credit approval. Credit or debit balances in a customer's account(s) may be offset by any other outstanding balance owed by or to the customer. Please allow 4 to 6 weeks for delivery. Offer available while quantities last.

Your Privacy—The Reader Service is committed to protecting your privacy. Our Privacy Policy is available online at www.ReaderService.com or upon request from the Reader Service.

We make a portion of our mailing list available to reputable third parties that offer products we believe may interest you. If you prefer that we not exchange your name with third parties, or if you wish to clarify or modify your communication preferences, please visit us at www.ReaderService.com/consumerschoice or write to us at Reader Service Preference Service, P.O. Box 9062, Buffalo, NY 14240-9062. Include your complete name and address.

HPLP15

LARGER-PRINT BOOKS!

GET 2 FREE LARGER-PRINT NOVELS PLUS

2 FREE GIFTS!

HARLEQUIN®

Romance

From the Heart, For the Heart

YES! Please send me 2 FREE LARGER-PRINT Harlequin® Romance novels and my 2 FREE gifts (gifts are worth about $10). After receiving them, if I don't wish to receive any more books, I can return the shipping statement marked "cancel." If I don't cancel, I will receive 4 brand-new novels every month and be billed just $5.09 per book in the U.S. or $5.49 per book in Canada. That's a savings of at least 15% off the cover price! It's quite a bargain! Shipping and handling is just 50¢ per book in the U.S. and 75¢ per book in Canada.* I understand that accepting the 2 free books and gifts places me under no obligation to buy anything. I can always return a shipment and cancel at any time. Even if I never buy another book, the two free books and gifts are mine to keep forever.

119/319 HDN GHWC

Name _____ (PLEASE PRINT) _____

Address _____ Apt. # _____

City _____ State/Prov. _____ Zip/Postal Code _____

Signature (if under 18, a parent or guardian must sign) _____

Mail to the **Reader Service:**
IN U.S.A.: P.O. Box 1867, Buffalo, NY 14240-1867
IN CANADA: P.O. Box 609, Fort Erie, Ontario L2A 5X3
Want to try two free books from another line?
Call 1-800-873-8635 or visit www.ReaderService.com.

* Terms and prices subject to change without notice. Prices do not include applicable taxes. Sales tax applicable in N.Y. Canadian residents will be charged applicable taxes. Offer not valid in Quebec. This offer is limited to one order per household. Not valid for current subscribers to Harlequin Romance Larger-Print books. All orders subject to credit approval. Credit or debit balances in a customer's account(s) may be offset by any other outstanding balance owed by or to the customer. Please allow 4 to 6 weeks for delivery. Offer available while quantities last.

Your Privacy—The Reader Service is committed to protecting your privacy. Our Privacy Policy is available online at www.ReaderService.com or upon request from the Reader Service.

We make a portion of our mailing list available to reputable third parties that offer products we believe may interest you. If you prefer that we not exchange your name with third parties, or if you wish to clarify or modify your communication preferences, please visit us at www.ReaderService.com/consumerchoice or write to us at Reader Service Preference Service, P.O. Box 9062, Buffalo, NY 14240-9062. Include your complete name and address.

HRLP11

LARGER-PRINT BOOKS!
GET 2 FREE LARGER-PRINT NOVELS PLUS
2 FREE GIFTS!

HARLEQUIN®
super romance®

More Story...More Romance

HSRLP15

WESTERN WP PROMISES

YES! Please send me **The Western Promises Collection** in Larger Print. This collection begins with 3 FREE books and 2 FREE gifts (gifts valued at approx. $14.00 retail) in the first shipment, along with the other first 4 books from the collection! If I do not cancel, I will receive 8 monthly shipments until I have the entire 51-book Western Promises collection. I will receive 2 or 3 FREE books in each shipment and I will pay just $4.99 US/ $5.89 CDN for each of the other four books in each shipment, plus $2.99 for shipping and handling per shipment. *If I decide to keep the entire collection, I'll have paid for only 32 books, because 19 books are FREE! I understand that accepting the 3 free books and gifts places me under no obligation to buy anything. I can always return a shipment and cancel at any time. My free books and gifts are mine to keep no matter what I decide.

272 HCN 3070 472 HCN 3070

Name	(PLEASE PRINT)	
Address		Apt. #
City	State/Prov.	Zip/Postal Code

Signature (if under 18, a parent or guardian must sign)

Mail to the **Reader Service**:

IN U.S.A.: P.O. Box 1867, Buffalo, NY 14240-1867
IN CANADA: P.O. Box 609, Fort Erie, Ontario L2A 5X3

* Terms and prices subject to change without notice. Prices do not include applicable taxes. Sales tax applicable in N.Y. Canadian residents will be charged applicable taxes. This offer is limited to one order per household. All orders subject to approval. Credit or debit balances in a customer's account(s) may be offset by any other outstanding balance owed by or to the customer. Please allow 4 to 6 weeks for delivery. Offer available while quantities last. Offer not available to Quebec residents.